M BELIEVE

A gripping crime thriller filled with twists

CATH STAINCLIFFE

Detective Janine Lewis Book 3

Revised edition 2022
Joffe Books, London
www.joffebooks.com

First published by Allison & Busby Limited
in Great Britain in 2013

This paperback edition was first published
in Great Britain in 2022

© Cath Staincliffe 2013, 2022

This book is a work of fiction. Names, characters,
businesses, organizations, places and events are either the
product of the author's imagination or are used fictitiously.
Any resemblance to actual persons, living
or dead, events or locales is entirely coincidental.
The spelling used is British English except where fidelity
to the author's rendering of accent or dialect supersedes
this. The right of Cath Staincliffe to be identified as
author of this work has been asserted in accordance with
the Copyright, Designs and Patents Act 1988.

Cover art by Nick Castle

ISBN: 978-1-80405-503-8

NOTE TO THE READER

Please note this book is set in the 2000s in England, a time before smartphones, and when social attitudes were very different.

PROLOGUE

Saturday 19 April

The playground in the park was busy, a result of the fine weather and an increase in popularity that had followed the recent council refurbishment. Sammy loved it here and for Claire it was a welcome respite. They'd been cooped up out of the rain too much these last few weeks. A three-year-old needed exercise, fresh air. Me too, thought Claire. Time was she and Clive would go off every weekend walking the Pennine Way or the Derbyshire Peaks. But once Sammy was born it didn't seem possible for them all to go. Claire knew some parents used backpacks and lugged their kids up hill and down dale but she and Clive had never really got into the habit. So today Clive had gone off on his own.

Claire waited while Sammy climbed the steps up to the top of the slide then she walked round to meet him, scooping him up as he shot off the end. She set him down and followed him back as he trotted to the steps. One o'clock, mid-April and it was actually warm. Claire called after him, 'Sammy, come here. Let's take your top off.' He jiggled on the spot eager to be playing as she unzipped the fleece and pulled it off him.

Up the steps he went and stood patiently on the top while the child ahead of him was coaxed down by her father. Claire took her place at the foot of the slide and Sammy slid down, stopping with a jolt near the end. His hands flew up to stop his glasses flying off. 'Whoops!' Claire said with a laugh, reassuring him that he'd no need to get upset.

She didn't mind Clive taking time out. Walking was a way for him to de-stress after the grind of the week's work and although they could have arranged a babysitter so she could accompany him, she preferred to save sitters for those precious evenings out, dinner with friends or a party. Clive had picked a glorious day for it, not a cloud in the sky, a slight breeze.

Sammy reached the top again, checked she was there and launched himself off. He'd learnt to lift his shoes off the surface so the friction wouldn't slow him down. He laughed with delight as he slid down and she felt a rush of love for him. She glanced at his nose, looking for any redness. She had put sunscreen on at the house; he was so very fair skinned she had to be extra careful. With his curly blonde hair he looked so sweet; sometimes he got mistaken for a girl. Claire wondered whether to suggest he try the swings or the climbing frame though she knew the slide was his favourite. He ran back.

There was a sudden blur of movement at her side and a shriek. Claire turned in time to see a little girl on the floor. She'd skinned her chin and was wailing, face red and contorted. Claire bent to help, lifting the child upright, murmuring words of comfort and scanning the crowd for the accompanying adult. Sure enough a man with an expression part humour, part dismay hoved into view, thanked Claire and lifted up the girl who threw her arms around his neck and bawled even louder.

Claire glanced over to the steps, looking for Sammy, blonde curls, chunky children's glasses, the distinctive red shoes. Claire's heart began to tighten as she realised he was not on the steps. She moved quickly to the front of the slide

2

where a plump boy in an infant Manchester United football strip clung to the top resisting exhortations to let go. Claire felt her heart kick and tug wildly as she whirled around, her eyes racing over the grass to the swings, to the roundabout and the climbing frame and back to the slide. A plea screamed in her head already, please, please let him be here. She began to call his name, increasingly frantic until other parents heard the rill of fear in her voice, saw the naked terror in her face and offered help. Claire described her son, words tumbling like stones, as her eyes darted around the park. She felt sick with nausea and her limbs, her neck and scalp were slick with sweat.

She climbed up on top of the wooden boat, the highest vantage point and scanned the playground again, shielding the glare from her eyes, calling all the while, 'Sammy, Sammy.' The atmosphere had changed, parents drew their children closer, some of them were looking in the shrubs that edged the area. Children stared up at her curiously; the weird lady shouting.

Heart thumping hard in her chest, she scoured the area, anticipating a glimpse of him: blonde hair, dinosaur T-shirt, the wonderful release and relief as she saw he was there, fine, unharmed, that all was right with the world.

Nothing.

Could he have gone home? Only a couple of hundred yards. He knew the way. She scrambled down. Should check the rest of the park first. She ran round the park twice more, trying to be systematic, but it was hard when the place was so crowded.

'Sammy,' she screamed, her voice becoming hoarse, 'Sammy, Sammy.' A tiny part of her brain observed all this almost dispassionately, hoping it was just a false alarm, that it would become an anecdote, a tale to offer at dinner parties and toddler group, self-deprecating, making out that she had been neurotic — her first child, an overreaction — imagining happy punch lines, he was by the bench all the time, he was playing hide and seek. But it was her body that knew the truth, not her brain, her body that was already turning from the park and sprinting towards their house, her body that was flooding her with adrenalin, that was spiking her blood pressure and making her mouth flood with saliva. Because whatever excuses her mind tried to present, her body knew.

Sammy had gone.

CHAPTER 1

Day One: Monday 18 April

Janine was about to leave, called to a suspicious death — she had the address but no further details — when Pete's car pulled up outside the house. She felt the familiar clench inside, wondered exactly when things were going to get easier with her ex or if it would always feel this way.

Two years ago he had left. Janine pregnant with Charlotte, their late unexpected addition to the family.

He'd made a clumsy attempt to invite himself back into the marriage not so long ago but Janine had told him straight that it couldn't work. They couldn't turn back time and she couldn't erase the sense of betrayal at his actions. Would it have been different if he had chosen to stay with Janine rather than move in with Tina? Might she have forgiven him the affair? Hard to tell and too late now anyway.

Eleanor and Tom climbed out of his car carrying backpacks. Both gave her a hurried wave and rushed into the house.

Pete didn't even stop the engine, just wound the window down as Janine approached. In a hurry no doubt. Like they all were, all the time. When did life become quite so frantic? Janine thought.

'Good weekend?' Janine said.

'Yep.' He nodded, slowly, repeatedly. God knows why.

'Did you take them out?'

'Yes. Cinema, pizza.' Almost monosyllabic. Like their teenager, Michael. Why was he behaving so oddly?

'Is everything OK?' she said, deciding to be direct. Perhaps he'd rowed with Tina, or the kids had done something irritating.

'Fine. Great,' he said. More nodding. 'Yes, fine. See you then.'

Janine, puzzled, watched him go. He hadn't even made time to pop in and see Charlotte having breakfast with the nanny, Vicky. That was sad. But then if he was running late maybe he just didn't have the time.

She called Richard Mayne, her DI, offered to give him a lift to the scene. She knew his car was in for repairs, he'd been complaining about it, the wait for parts.

'Er, no,' he said stammering a little, 'you're fine.'

'You risking the bus?'

'No, I . . . er . . . I'm sorted.'

'See you there, then.' Why was everyone being so weird today?

* * *

The crime scene cordon on the residential street had been set about fifty yards from the address where the body had been found. 16 Kendal Avenue. The place was a hubbub of activity, crime scene vans were within the cordon and outside the house itself. Neighbours stood in twos and threes speculating with each other. As Janine pulled on her protective suit, another car arrived, her colleague Richard Mayne in the passenger seat. And look who's driving, Millie Saunders from the press office. Janine watched Richard kiss Millie on the cheek before getting out and waving her off.

'Hi.' Richard came over, 'Have you got a spare suit?' Janine stared at him, eyebrows raised in question.

Richard rolled his eyes at her, gave a laugh, sighed. 'Millie Saunders,' he said, 'press office. Satisfied?'

'Was she?' Janine said dryly. Richard laughed. She turned and picked another suit out of the stash she carried with her in the car boot and passed it to him.

Janine felt the teensiest pinch of jealousy. Unfair she knew. Richard and her were mates, that's all. Work partners and pals. Yes, there was an attraction, they flirted with each other now and again but would never take it further and risk ruining their friendship. Janine had the odd fantasy — he was gorgeous, tall, dark, and the rest. But that's all it was, fantasy.

When he was ready they approached the officer in charge of cordon, showed her their warrant cards and walked up the road.

'Not a bad area,' Richard remarked.

Janine agreed. Large, solidly built, semi-detached houses, the sort with decent sized gardens and enough roof space to make conversions. Some sort of improvement was going on at this place, a skip on the pavement, rubble and debris in the front garden, windows boarded up, bricks stacked at the far end of the drive. An inner cordon was rigged up around the driveway where a white tent had been erected to preserve the scene. Janine introduced herself and Richard to the crime scene manager, a man called John Trenton.

'Young child,' Trenton said, 'in the main drain.' He led them into the tent where there was a manhole, rectangular, nothing visible but murky water. Sammy Wray? Janine's first thought. The city was awash with posters of the three-year-old missing for the past nine days. Sammy's picture photo-shopped to include the clothes he'd last been seen in and the heading, 'Have You Seen This Child?' Each time she'd driven past one of them Janine had felt a surge of sympathy for his parents, for the unimaginable horror they must be living through. And the professional in her knew that with the time that had elapsed the probability was that if Sammy Wray was ever found he would not be alive.

'Sammy Wray?' she said aloud.

'Could well be. The size of the body is right,' Trenton said, 'the T-shirt.'

She glanced at Richard, his face set for a moment, then his eyes met hers, a look of trepidation and resignation. This will be a hard one. Child murders always were, grim and heartbreaking.

'Looks like a blow to the head,' Trenton said, 'impact to the back of the skull.'

'We'll get the parents to ID him?' said Janine.

'Too distressing,' Trenton replied. 'The effects of the water, and animals.' He cleared his throat. 'An appalling scenario for all concerned.' He held up a video camera, 'Would you . . .?' he invited.

Janine nodded.

She watched the shaky footage. The scene in the drainage tunnel lit garishly. The camera panned up the sewer a couple of feet to reveal the bundle, a white sheet torn and stained, the mess that had once been a little boy. She swallowed.

'Pathologist on their way,' Trenton said.

'Good,' though there was no doubt in anybody's mind that this was a suspicious death.

'Who alerted us?' Janine said.

'Flood reported by the neighbours at the other side.' He gestured towards the adjoining house. 'The Palfreys. They called the builders, thinking it might have something to do with them, a blockage or whatever. Builder came out and called the utility company. When the water guy goes down he finds the body.'

'The water's gone down now,' Richard said.

'Yes, flash flood apparently, old drains, they're too narrow to cope with the run off and we'd several inches of rainfall in the early hours.'

'We'll speak to the parents. Fast track the DNA,' Janine said. I don't want them waiting a minute longer.'

They set off immediately. She was eager to reach the Wrays before they heard any whisper of the morning's discovery. On the way, she alerted Lisa, one of her detective constables, asked her to start setting up an incident room and to call in the rest of the team. Then she spoke briefly to the officer who had been co-ordinating the missing child operation, informed him of the discovery and got an overview of their investigation to date.

CHAPTER 2

The Wrays' house, a well-appointed Edwardian terrace, stood on Foley Road, a stone's throw away from Withington Park where Sammy Wray had last been seen and about half a mile from the Kendal Avenue crime scene.

At the front door Janine took a moment, bracing herself for what was to come. Richard waited, then gave a rueful smile, cocked his head. Ready? Janine nodded and he knocked on the door, three loud raps.

Claire Wray opened the door, her husband Clive close behind her and at his side a woman who was acting as their family liaison officer, Sue Quinn.

'Mr and Mrs Wray, I'm DCI Janine Lewis.'

Claire's eyes darted between Janine and Richard as if searching for something but Janine could tell Claire knew, even before she spoke, fear quaking in her voice. 'You've found him?' She knew. After all it had been nine days, nine days waiting for this knock at the door, expecting redemption at first, living on crazy hope and air, then nerves shattered and sleep deprived, craving any news, anything at all.

Claire sought the answer in Janine's expression, in the silence, and understood. Her face crumpled.

'Can we come inside?' Janine said gently.

The house was stylish, clean lines and natural materials, wood floors, a slate hearth. Framed landscape photographs hung on the walls, some child's drawings too. Clive was a graphic designer, ran a small firm. Claire did French translation for an import company.

Janine watched Claire clutch at a small navy fleece on the arm of the sofa and hug it to herself as she sat down. Sammy's, Janine assumed. Totem. Security blanket.

Clive hovered, coiled, tense.

Janine told them what she had to. 'I am so sorry. I'm here to tell you that we've recovered a boy's body matching Sammy's description.'

'Get out,' Clive Wray yelled. A normal reaction, Janine had come across it often before, shooting the messenger.

Claire bent double, crying out, 'God, no. No.'

'Get out,' Clive wheeled around.

Janine continued calmly, 'It's terrible news, I know.'

Claire was sobbing, howling really.

Janine exchanged glances with Richard, some mutual support in a harrowing situation. After a few moments she indicated he should pick up the thread.

'Until we have the DNA result, to confirm identity,' Richard said, 'we will not be releasing Sammy's name.'

'Why can't we identify him?' Clive said.

'I'm afraid there is extensive damage to the body,' Richard said.

'Oh, God,' Claire looked up, her face blotchy with tears. 'Where did you find him? Where was he?'

It was important to be honest but sometimes it just felt like pouring salt into the wounds, thought Janine. 'The victim was found in a drainage tunnel, at a property in Withington.'

Claire whimpered and Clive turned away from them.

Sue came in bringing a tray of tea. She placed it on the coffee table and then stood at the back of the room, unobtrusively.

'Sue will carry on as your family liaison officer and she'll remain with you,' Janine said. 'I'm now going to be leading the investigation and DI Mayne will be working with me.'

11

Clive Wray passed Claire a drink but her hand was shaking too badly to take hold of it.

'I know you've already made statements to the missing person's inquiry but as circumstances have changed we need to look at everything again. Can we do that now? Or we can take a break and come back later,' Janine said.

'Now,' Claire Wray said.

'Claire?' Clive looked at her, obviously concerned for her emotional state.

'Now,' Claire said again, steel in her voice. Was it just determination or was some of that metal directed at her husband? The loss of a child often tore relationships apart. Was that already happening for the Wrays?

Janine nodded her agreement and opened her briefcase, got out her daybook to record notes. Clive sat down beside his wife on the sofa.

'Can you describe for me what Sammy was wearing on the Saturday he went missing?' Janine said.

'His navy trousers, a dinosaur T-shirt. Red shoes.' She looked at Janine, a flicker of hope, as if Janine would suddenly tell her those didn't fit with what they had found. Janine didn't evade that look but she answered it with one of regret.

'You went to the park,' Richard prompted her.

'About quarter to one. He loves the slide. One minute he was—' she faltered. 'I only turned round for a minute and he was gone.'

'Then you raised the alarm,' Richard said.

Claire said, 'Yes. I looked round the park, I ran back here. There was no sign and I called the police.'

Richard turned to Clive, 'And you arrived home—?'

'At four. The police were here, I couldn't . . . you never imagine . . .' he said as if re-living the shock of it. Then the reality of the new nightmare hit him. 'Oh, God.'

'You'd been walking?' said Janine.

'Up Kinder Scout, Hayfield,' Clive said.

'On your own?'

'Yes.'

'Can you think of anyone who could verify that?' Janine said.

There was a horrible silence and Clive Wray stared at her as he recognised the implication behind the question.

'It would help us eliminate you from the inquiry,' she said, 'I realise that may seem insensitive but it is routine procedure. If you can think of anybody—'

'No,' he said quickly, 'it was pretty quiet. I passed a few other walkers but they were strangers. I've no idea how you'd contact them.'

Claire started crying again. Clive Wray made a move to comfort her, his arm reaching out but she froze at his touch, shrank away and he let his arm fall.

* * *

Leaving the Wrays, as Janine was putting her case in the back of the car she found one of Charlotte's shoes there, and some crayons. For a giddy moment Janine imagined Charlotte lost, missing, hurt. There but for the . . . No point in dwelling on it. Janine's job now was to use all her professional skill and that of her team to find out who killed Sammy Wray. And her integrity, her dedication was all she could offer the Wrays. Empathy yes but not sentimentality.

'Odd atmosphere, didn't you think? Lot of tension,' said Janine.

'What d'you expect?' Richard said.

'Not directed at us, though; with each other,' she said.

'Could have been having problems before this,' Richard said. 'Don't they reckon having a child stresses a relationship?'

Sure does. Janine knew how the business of sharing the care of children was fertile ground for spats and resentment between her and Pete both before and after the separation. That old chestnut of both people working full-time but the woman also doing the bulk of the parenting and the housework. Did Claire still work full-time now they had Sammy? Maybe she was a stay-at-home mum. All the family background would be in the files from the missing person case. She'd have to get up to speed on it to brief her team.

'Maybe she blames Clive for not being there,' Richard said.

'Or he blames Claire for losing Sammy,' Richard said.

'Yes,' she said. Janine's stomach flipped over as she remembered one time when she had lost Tom. She had taken the kids to the Trafford centre. It was BT (before Tina as she thought of it) and BC (before Charlotte). Eleanor had helped herself to some sparkly crayons in the stationery shop, which Janine only realised once they had moved on to the gaming place. Michael was absorbed in playing the games and Janine told Tom to stay with his big brother while she took Eleanor to give back the stolen goods.

On their return, with Eleanor bawling, Janine found Michael, slack jawed and glazed eyes, trying a shoot-em-up game, and no sign of Tom.

Janine's blood had turned to ice. Tom was found, none the worse for wear, after the security staff were alerted and announcements made. He'd gone looking for candy floss.

Pete never blamed her, not for that, but she blamed herself. Pete's blame centred on how much her job impacted on her time at home. But Janine loved her job, just as she loved her kids, and refused to let Pete guilt trip her about it. She could do that all by herself on a bad day, thank you very much.

CHAPTER 3

While the incident room was being set up, Janine famil-
iarised herself with the files on Sammy Wray. She passed
eyewitness statements from the park to her sergeants, Shap
and Butchers, to read and asked Richard to liaise with the
crime scene manager and the CSIs for any information
emerging from the scene. Then Janine attended the post
mortem.

There was an understandable pathos to the sight of such
a small figure on the table.

'No trousers, no shoes,' Janine observed as the pathologist's assistant photographed the child first wrapped in the
torn sheet, then with the sheet removed in just T-shirt and
underpants.

'No, no socks either,' the pathologist said.

All sorts of debris had clung to the sheet and the
exposed parts of the victim from the filthy sewer water.

Janine waited patiently while more photographs were
taken and notes made of the external appearance of the
child. X-rays were taken too before the internal examination
began. Janine was there for confirmation of the cause of
death and she soon got her answer. A substantial fracture to
the back of the skull had killed the child.

'It's over a wide area, so we're looking at impact with a large item,' the pathologist said.

'A brick?' Janine asked, thinking of where the body was found, the building materials to hand.

'Don't think so, no linear edge and no brick dust in the scalp which I'd expect. I've seen injuries like this before with falls or where a child's been swung against the wall.'

Janine steadied herself. 'So, we're not looking for a weapon as such?'

'No.'

'Any sign of sexual abuse?'

'No.'

'The other damage?' Janine said.

'I've more tests to do but I'd say almost certainly post-mortem, and all consistent with the site where the victim was found, the sewer.'

That was something, Janine thought. Whoever had snatched Sammy Wray had not tortured or raped him.

'If you find any trace material on the body that might be significant, will you let me know straightaway?' Janine said.

* * *

Butchers had only nipped out for a butty but when he returned his heart sank. His desk was decorated with helium balloons, a joke gallows and noose and an inflatable plastic diamond ring. It was common knowledge then.

He should never have mentioned it to Shap. In fact he never intended to but Shap had a way of worming things out of a person, tricking you into saying more than you intended. A handy talent for a copper, but a pain in the arse when you were the fall guy who found all your best kept secrets dragged into the light for all to see.

Shap's eyes lit up as he saw Butchers was back and he said, 'She called it off yet? You wanna get the rock back if she does, mate. Stick that in the pre-nuptials.'

'Who've you told?' Butchers said. 'Have you told everyone?'

DI Mayne and DCI Lewis chose that moment to walk through the room. Butchers sat down quickly hoping to evade attention but he heard Richard Mayne say to the boss, loud enough for the whole room to hear, 'Someone finally said yes to Butchers.'

'Anyone actually met her?' the boss said.

'Mail order, eh, i'nt she?' Shap cackled. 'Twenty eight days money back guarantee.'

Butchers grinned, feeling sick. Brilliant. Totally. Brilliant.

* * *

Bang on time at ten-thirty and Janine's boss, Detective Superintendent Louise Hogg came in, Millie Saunders at her elbow. Janine glanced at Richard in curiosity. He gave a shrug, no idea why his new squeeze was at the briefing. Staff were still busy setting up computers and extra phone lines.

Detective Superintendent Hogg stepped up to the boards, which contained photographs from the scene at Kendal Avenue, notes of evidence, summary of the post-mortem report, a map of the area, pictures of the sheet and the clothes. At one side — linked by a dotted line — were the details of Sammy Wray's abduction, nine days earlier, and a question mark beside his photo.

'A small boy, killed and left in a drainage tunnel. It's the sort of case we pray won't happen,' Hogg said. 'If anyone needs to step down at any point — do it. Counselling likewise. I don't want to lose you.' She surveyed the team for a moment. 'Now, most of you know Millie Saunders, press office. It's a high-profile case, and Millie will be developing and managing our press strategy.'

Millie gave a nod of the head, by way of greeting. She was slim, dark haired, extremely attractive and always impeccably turned out. She was bright too, quick thinking, Janine knew. She had to be in her role — a link between the media who were always ravenous for news and the police inquiry. As press officer she had to act quickly to make sure the right information reached the right people at the best time and that adverse publicity was kept to a minimum.

'Janine?' Louise Hogg stepped away, inviting her to take over.

'We have three lines of inquiry,' Janine said, 'the family, the park and the crime scene. The post-mortem shows death due to a fractured skull consistent with a fall or collision with a large flat surface, a wall for example. There's no sign of sexual abuse. The child was wrapped in a sheet, generic poly-cotton, chain stores carry them, catalogues. Clothes as per description: popular high street range.' Janine pointed to the photograph from the poster-appeal and to the recent images of the tattered T-shirt taken from the child's body. 'But footwear, socks and trousers are still missing. Estimated time of death is at least a week ago but that is only an estimate. We do not at present know where the primary crime scene, and by that I mean the site of death, is. The property at Kendal Avenue is being examined. The pathologist reported two hairs found on the body, short, straight, brown so not belonging to the boy,' Janine said. 'OK, ideas: family?'

'The Wrays kill him then they report him missing as a cover up,' Shap said. 'Kendal Avenue, that's only a few streets away from the Wrays' house.' Everyone knew the statistics, inside out and upside down. Eighty-eight percent of victims knew their killers. For kids it was even higher.

'But Claire was seen at the park with Sammy,' Janine said.

'Clive's got a dodgy alibi though: no-one to verify where he was,' Richard said.

'Claire didn't see anyone making off with the child,' Janine said.

'She was distracted and whoever did it moved quickly and had the advantage of the slide obscuring them from view,' Richard pointed out.

'Unless she's covering for him,' said Shap.

People did sometimes, Janine knew only too well, they were persuaded into deceit because they were too fearful to tell the truth, or because they were complicit in the behaviour that led to a death, or because they believed the murderer, who said it was an accident, or a mistake, or a moment's folly. But a child, an only child, she found it hard to credit that Claire Wray would do such a thing. The woman was heart-broken, it didn't seem plausible that she'd be able to maintain any fiction about events.

And Clive? Clive felt harder to read. Janine sensed some-thing off-key, small but resonant when they talked to him, as though there was some other business claiming part of his attention.

'Then why draw attention like that?' Janine said. 'Why not hide the whole thing instead of crying abduction? If she was colluding, she wouldn't have raised the alarm.'

'Perhaps Claire only discovered later that Clive was involved. Yet chose to stand by him,' said Butchers.

Janine shook her head. It didn't mesh with what she'd seen of Claire so far.

'So Clive does it on his own. Grab the kid, turn and walk away. Pretends it's a game: let's hide from mummy,' Shap said.

'Suppose he was involved — why bury Sammy so close to home?' Janine indicated the locations on the map.

'Opportunistic?' said Lisa.

'Perhaps,' Janine said. 'Can we examine that lack of an alibi? Shap, get onto the wardens, park rangers whatever. See if they can help. CCTV between here and Hayfield, speed cameras. Anything that'll flag up Clive Wray.'

Shap gave a groan and Janine saw Butchers gloat at the mention of CCTV, it was a tedious task at the best of times.

Janine saw Louise Hogg nod approval and gave herself a mental pat on the back. She didn't usually have the boss in on her briefings and it always unsettled her, though of course, Hogg was a far better prospect than her former boss Keith Hackett who had taken great delight at undermining her at every turn.

Janine gestured to the whiteboards. 'Moving on — the crime scene. The Kendal Avenue property is being refurbished. We'll be talking to the contractors. Butchers, you lead door-to-door with the neighbours. Why this place? We know the child was already dead when he was put in the drain. Was it simply handy? People panic when they kill. Most murders aren't meticulously planned and executed; people have to improvise. Perhaps the manhole on Kendal Avenue is simply the first hiding place the killer found for the body.'

Richard held up a report. 'From CSIs, a screw from a pair of glasses fell from the sheet as the body was recovered. We also have fragments of optical glass on the pavement near the manhole cover.'

'Sammy had his glasses on at the park,' Janine said.

There was a moment's quiet as everyone absorbed that — the evidence reinforcing the possibility that this child was the missing boy.

Janine looked at the boards, the photograph of the child, the round glasses.

'The sheet,' Lisa said, 'well, it's like a shroud, isn't it?'

Janine considered this, nodded at Lisa to elaborate.

'Not just dumped in a bin bag.'

'A mark of respect?' said Janine.

'Or he just grabbed what was at hand,' Richard said.

'Yes. OK, now the park,' said Janine, one eye on the clock. She had a press conference to front. She gestured to the section on the whiteboards that detailed information on the abduction. 'Sammy Wray was abducted, on Saturday the nineteenth of April shortly after one pm. Plenty of reports of Sammy and Claire, of him playing on the slide. Claire stops to help a child who's tripped up and that's when Sammy disappears. All this is confirmed by independent witnesses. Butchers?'

'We're reviewing eyewitness statements but to date no-one saw the actual abduction.'

Richard checked the board. 'Three sightings were cross-referenced but not yet traced?' he said.

'Yep,' said Shap. 'We still need to trace a woman on her own, an elderly couple with a dog and a bearded man seen acting strangely by the swings.'

Somebody groaned and Louise Hogg spoke up, 'I know there's always a bearded weirdo acting strangely but don't dismiss it completely.'

'You all clear what you're working on?' Janine asked. Nods and agreement. People were eager to get cracking, to get the investigation up to full steam. 'As always details remain confidential and we'll be keeping to the basic known facts for this morning's press conference. Lots to do,' she said, 'let's get on with it.'

People dispersed. Millie whispered something to Richard and he roared with laughter. Janine tried to hide her irritation. 'Millie?'

Richard hesitated a moment but Janine waited until he moved away before speaking. 'Can we avoid sensationalising it?'

'Do my best,' Millie said, 'but the nationals will be onto it, the Sundays. Big story.' She checked her watch. 'You ready?'

* * *

In the conference room, Millie stood at the front observing while Janine stepped up to the table to address the journalists. As soon as Janine opened her mouth, a battery of flashlights went off.

Janine took a breath and then spoke directly to the crowd. 'At approximately eight o'clock this morning, police were called to Kendal Avenue, in Withington, where the body of a young child was recovered from a drainage tunnel. Cause of death was a fracture to the skull. We are not yet in a position to confirm identity.'

'Is it Sammy Wray?' one of the journalists called out. Not local, perhaps up from London.

'We've not made a positive identification yet but we are investigating that possibility,' Janine said, choosing her words with care. 'We still have individuals we would like to talk to who were at Withington Park on the nineteenth of April and who we have not yet spoken to. I would ask those people to contact us as soon as possible. We would also ask anyone with information, anyone who saw or heard anything on Kendal Avenue, anyone who thinks they know something, no matter how small, that might help the inquiry, to please come forward, contact your local police station or ring the police helpline. In cases like this the help of the general public is invaluable.'

Hands went up and people shouted questions but it had already been made clear that Janine would not be answering any questions after the official statement. She nodded by way of thanks, turned and followed Millie out of the room.

CHAPTER 4

Butchers, on door-to-door, had spoken first to the Palfreys at number 14, across the driveway from the empty house where the body had been found. They had reported the flood but had absolutely nothing else to offer, though they were helpful as could be. Both retired local government workers, they were distressed at the events unfolding on their doorstep and appeared guilty that they hadn't seen or heard anything untoward that Butchers could write down.

Second on his list were the Staffords number 18, the property adjoining the house. It was mid-afternoon and Butchers knocked several times before the door was opened by a middle aged man with a monk's tonsure and a sour look on his face. The householder was in pyjamas.

'What?' he demanded.

'Mr Ken Stafford? DS Butchers, you're aware of the incident next door?'

'Yes.'

'We're interviewing everyone in the vicinity,' Butchers said.

'Can't help you. I didn't see anything.' Ken Stafford shut the door.

Butchers felt a flare of impatience. Mardy-arse. They'd a little kiddie dead in the house next-door and this idiot was being awkward about talking to the police.

Butchers hammered a tattoo on the door again, twice. He wasn't going anywhere until he'd got what he came for.

With a show of irritation, Ken Stafford let him in.

Inside, the living room was cluttered and dusty. The video game cases littering the carpet in front of the TV and console and a pair of battered skater-boy shoes in the middle of the room suggested a teenager lived there too.

Butchers took in the photos, also dusty, on the wall. Mum, dad and child, a boy.

'Can I talk to your wife, as well?' Butchers said.

Ken Stafford took his time replying, 'She died.'

Butchers cleared his throat, 'Sorry.' He indicated the photos. 'And the boy?'

'Luke, at school.'

'You say you've not seen anything suspicious.' Butchers opened his notebook. 'What about regular comings and goings?'

The man shrugged, no.

'Neighbours, builders?'

'Builders, that's a joke,' Ken Stafford said caustically. 'Permanent go-slow. Don't see them for days then they turn up at the crack of dawn. I work nights. But they don't give a toss.'

'Can you remember when you last saw them?' Butchers said.

'A week ago. The Monday, McEvoy was around. Is that it?'

There was a noise from the hall and someone came in, shutting the door so hard the whole house rattled.

The lad stood in the doorway, slight, skinny, dark hair, he'd piercings on his face among the angry-looking acne. 'Luke?' said Butchers.

'The police,' Ken Stafford said, 'want to know if we saw anything.'

Luke Stafford shrugged. 'No,' he said, 'just the coppers and that this morning.'

Butchers spent another ten minutes with the Staffords but made no further progress, nothing he could take back to the inquiry. They were both miserable buggers, the lad you could understand, embarrassed at that age to be asked anything, but the father Ken, curt and short-tempered, just seemed bitter. 'If you do remember anything,' Butchers said, as he was leaving, 'seeing anything, hearing anything in the last ten days, please let us know.'

'Is it Sammy Wray?' the kid said, his face flaming red, when Butchers moved to the hallway.

'Waiting to confirm identity,' Butchers said. The standard reply.

* * *

Work at Kendal Avenue was being carried out by a local builder Donny McEvoy and his mate Joe Breeley. Donny McEvoy had come out to the site when the flood was reported and had been there when the body was recovered. He'd left details where he could be contacted with the police.

The site was in Gorton, a tract of land that had been cleared of old warehousing and was now being re-developed for small, industrial units. Janine and Richard made their way to the office and Richard asked the site manager for Donny McEvoy. The manager pointed to the far side of the yard where a man was operating a cement mixer.

As they reached him, he pulled off his gloves. A fine coating of cement dust had settled in the lines on his face, his eyebrows and glasses giving him an almost comical appearance. He pulled off his specs, rubbed at them with his fingers.

'Donny McEvoy,' said Richard.

'Yeah. This about the murder?' His eyes lit up.

'That's right,' said Richard.

'I was there — when they found him,' McEvoy said. 'Huge shock. Have you got any leads? They reckon most cases like this, it's the family.'

'When were you last working there?' Janine said.

25

'Last Monday, the twenty-first,' said McEvoy. 'Mate called in sick so I've been filling in here since.' He leaned in closer to them. 'The child, he'd been there a while, hadn't he?'

'How come you were there this morning?' Janine said ignoring the man's question.

'Called out when the neighbours saw the flooding. Was me got the water company in.'

'Did you notice anything that might help us?' Richard said, 'Either today or at any time in the past nine days.'

'Nine days,' McEvoy nodded his head as if wise to some great secret. 'That's 'cos you think it's Sammy Wray, isn't it? Nine days since he was snatched.'

The avid gleam in his eyes, the spit that glistened at the corners of his mouth revolted Janine. He was a ghoul, one of those amateur sleuths who liked to think they could compete with the police, who got a prurient kick from being close to sudden violent death. Was it any more than that? McEvoy had access to the drains. Had he any previous form? Her mind was running ahead, something she cautioned in her officers. Gather the details, steadily, precisely, then analyse.

'Did you notice anything?' Janine said, coldly.

McEvoy shook his head. 'I've been wracking my brains. And it was a fractured skull,' he said swiftly, 'do you know if he was killed somewhere else and moved? There was this case in Florida—'

Janine held up her hands to stop him. 'Thank you Mr McEvoy. If you do think of anything that may be significant please get in touch with the inquiry. Where can we find Mr Breeley?'

* * *

Joe Breeley was outside his council house working on a maroon Vauxhall Astra with the bonnet raised. Janine took in the neglected front garden, grass and long weeds, a pallet and some bags of sand, a white van parked alongside the car.

'Not too sick to play mechanic,' Richard said as they went to greet him.

'Joe Breeley? DCI Lewis.' Janine introduced herself as the man raised his head from over the engine.

'DI Mayne.' Richard showed his warrant card.

'You may have heard the body of a child was recovered from the site where you are working on Kendal Avenue,' Janine said.

Joe nodded. 'Saw the news,' he said. He closed the car bonnet. 'Terrible.'

'Could we have a word inside?' she said.

He wiped his hands on the front of his jeans and took them into the house.

'I couldn't believe it,' Breeley said leading the way into the living room. 'Mandy, it's the police. They've come about that little kiddie. Here, sit down,' he said, clearing a pile of children's clothes off the settee.

'It's horrible,' Mandy said. She was winding a baby, rubbing at its back, the empty bottle of feed on the side table. Janine guessed she was in her early twenties, a little dishevelled. Probably too busy with the baby to get time for herself.

The room was scattered with toys, more baby clothes draped over the large fireguard in front of the gas fire. Daytime TV was on but Joe Breeley muted it with the remote. On the walls Janine saw the family photos, Joe and Mandy and two children. A good looking family, the children fair like their mother. Mandy was attractive, slim with huge eyes and long, fine hair.

'How long have you been at the site?' Richard said.

'Six weeks, it's a big job. Place needed gutting,' said Breeley.

'And when were you last there?'

'Week last Saturday. Till lunchtime,' he said.

Janine heard the rising wail of a child from upstairs.

Mandy got to her feet. 'You take him,' she said to Breeley and handed the baby over to him. 'Our John,' she explained, 'miserable with chickenpox.'

Janine groaned in sympathy, Charlotte had it only last month, it had gone round the neighbourhood like wildfire, left her little girl with three pockmarks on her face despite Janine's best attempts to stop her scratching.

Mandy left them.

'And who's this?' Janine nodded at the baby.

Joe Breeley smiled, 'Aidan.'

'Did you see anyone acting suspiciously, or anyone close to the main drainage?' Richard said.

'Is that where they found him?' Joe Breeley frowned. 'Christ! When you've kids of your own, you . . .' He shook his head. 'No. No-one,' he answered.

'You're not at work today?' Janine said.

'Bad back,' he grimaced.

He'd looked fine bent over the car Janine thought. She glanced at Richard, sharing her scepticism and they waited it out.

Joe Breeley sighed, looked slightly shamefaced as he added, 'Well, weather like we've been having. The rain — takes twice as long to do a job. And with John being ill . . . We'll finish on time. Get paid by results.' Then it seemed to dawn on him that no work would be happening at Kendal Avenue for some time to come, in the light of events. 'Course . . . now . . .' he faltered.

Mandy came back in and took Aidan from Breeley. The baby had drifted off and didn't wake as she lifted him up and cuddled him.

'Last Saturday,' said Janine, 'what time did you start work?'

'Just after nine.'

'And lunchtime was when?' she said.

'One-ish. Came back here,' Breeley said.

'And that afternoon?' Janine said.

Joe Breeley gave a shrug. 'We just did stuff in the house.'

Mandy gave a small laugh. 'He's that busy fixing other people's houses, I'm always on at him to sort this place out.'

'Was there ever any sign of intruders in the property, anything odd like that?' Richard said.

'No, nothing,' Breeley said.

'If you do think of anything that might help please get in touch,' Richard said, 'anything at all.'

Breeley nodded.

'It's awful,' Mandy said again and hugged Aidan tighter as if she was anxious to keep him safe.

CHAPTER 5

Claire Wray felt numb, crushed by the dreadful news. It was as though she had been pulled frozen from the cold sea, no sensation anywhere beyond a gnawing dark ache in every muscle, deep in her bones.

Her mind stumbled around knocking into memories of Sammy: his birth over-shadowed by the theatrical antics of Clive's ex Felicity who had claimed the spotlight with a cruelly timed suicide bid; their worries when they first realised Sammy couldn't see properly and all the worst scenarios of blindness or worse plagued them until the tests had all come back and it was known to be simply short-sightedness; Sammy's passion for tractors and diggers and steam-rollers; the slight lisp he had; the feel of his hand in hers.

Then her thoughts would trip over the grim facts, the drainage tunnel, a sewer, her baby in a sewer. Preposterous. Life wasn't meant to go like this. Sammy was supposed to grow and thrive, become a schoolboy, a teenager, a man. All those futures.

She shuffled on the sofa, pressed Sammy's fleece to her cheek. Who would do such a thing?

At the back of her skull she felt the tingle of unease, the mistrust that had been growing there ever since Sammy had gone. And Clive had come home.

Something about Clive's manner, almost imperceptible but a taint of distance, of awkwardness, she could sense even in her distress and anguish. He was holding back. He was guarded.

At first she took it to be Clive's way of masking his criticism of her, of hiding how he blamed her. She had lost sight of Sammy and Sammy had been taken. Her watch. Her fault.

Clive was a good man, she believed that, a kind man. He rarely raised his voice, she had never seen him lash out, couldn't imagine him being violent. But perhaps he was a little too kind. Weak. Like the way he fell for Felicity's stunts time and again, instead of accepting that he couldn't be held responsible for her actions.

But as the days had gone on, interminable and tense, as they had waited for sightings, for leads, for fresh appeals, as Sammy's disappearance fell from the news bulletins and front pages, Claire began to wonder whether Clive was — too hard to put into words, something so foul, so unnatural. He loved Sammy. He was walking that day, wasn't he? If only he'd gone with a friend then she wouldn't even be thinking like this. But he'd been alone, unaccounted for, if you like. And that reserve in him had not eased; if anything it had grown stronger. While Claire blabbed about everything she could, dredging up memories from the park, keen to colour in every last detail, Clive's responses to the police and investigators was always vague, muted, minimal.

She didn't like the way her mind was working. Perhaps it was a distraction, a defensive thing, if she was fretting over Clive it diverted her from facing the probable truth about Sammy. That he was dead. That he was never coming back. He would never need new shoes again. She would never hold him in her arms again.

Clive came in then. 'I'm going up,' he said quietly. 'You want anything?'

She shook her head.

'Sue said she'd sort out some shopping tomorrow, should be back here mid-morning.'

Like I care, Claire thought. Then felt uncharitable as tears burnt her eyes. Sue was only trying to support them and Clive was just passing on the message. 'OK,' she said.

He made no move to touch her, to give her a goodnight kiss but turned and went. Just as well, really, she would only have rebuffed him. Her body language communicated what she'd not been able to articulate, that she mistrusted him.

She listened as Clive made his way upstairs. She heard the creak of the floor in their bedroom above.

I can check, she thought, *put an end to all these stupid fantasies and then concentrate on Sammy, on what really matters. Probably find out I'm wrong, that Clive was doing exactly what he said he was and this is just him knocked sideways by the abduction.* Easy enough to look. It had been wet for weeks before that Saturday. One reason why the park had been so busy, the fine weather was a relief. It had rained again since, the good spell only lasted a couple of days. People were talking about the wettest spring on record. Where had Sammy been then? When the rain came back? All those days since? Wet and cold, somewhere? Hungry? Or by then had he—

She wrenched her train of thought back to Clive. The ground would have been waterlogged, wouldn't it? He'd put dubbing on his boots the day before, she knew because Sammy had been asking a stream of questions: what was it, why, could he have some on his shoes?

Claire listened again for any movement upstairs and then, satisfied, got to her feet. She felt hollow and shaky, as though she had flu. She went through to the utility room at the back of the house and switched on the light, pausing again and listening. No sound from above.

His boots were on the bottom of the rack. She lifted them, they were heavier than she expected. She turned them over. No mud in the cleats, nothing. She examined the uppers, a uniform dull sheen on the brown leather from the dubbing. No new cuts or scrapes, no smears of dirt.

Her stomach dropped and a clammy sweat erupted all over her skin. It doesn't prove anything, she tried to tell herself. But a voice was clamouring in her head: he's lying, you know he's lying.

Was he? Perhaps he'd taken a route that was paved, avoided the boggy parts and the rough tracks that criss-crossed the great peak. But she knew herself from walking there with him how few sections were paved. Any halfway decent walk meant navigating peat bogs and gullies, fording streams and tramping through heather and bracken.

She put the boots back. His Barbour jacket was hanging on the pegs. Her hands trembling she felt in the pockets. A tissue in the left, a piece of paper in the right. Folded. She opened it out. A flyer, and a parking ticket tucked inside. The leaflet read, *Sports Bonanza. Sport City. All welcome.* She was about to dismiss it as the sort of thing left on the car under the windscreen wiper, until she noticed the date. *Saturday April 19th.*

The same date on the parking ticket.

She felt her heart kick and skip a beat.

April 19th. Sport City.

She couldn't bear to think what this meant beyond knowing that Clive had lied. *Oh God.* She perched on the buffet in the corner, shivering, her pulse galloping. She stared at Clive's jacket, at her own hanging beside it, at the lower row of pegs for Sammy's things. Her eyes blurred with tears.

Why would he lie?

She would tell the police. She had to. For Sammy.

CHAPTER 6

Michael, her eldest son, had agreed to feed the kids and for that Janine was so grateful. She would clear up, couldn't expect him to do that as well. Vicky, the nanny had gone out, didn't work evenings, except by prior arrangement and with lots of notice, but she would have put Charlotte to bed before leaving.

After Janine had taken off her coat and slipped off her shoes she went into the kitchen, catching the tail end of conversation.

'Charlotte will be two and you'll be ten,' Eleanor was telling her little brother, and I'll be thirteen.'

'It's still warm,' Michael told Janine, nodding at the remnants of a lasagne.

'It's bound to have dark hair,' Eleanor went on.

'Wonderful,' Janine thanked Michael and sat down next to Tom. 'Shove up,' she said, 'make room for a little one.'

Michael passed her a plate of food.

'Why?' Tom said to Eleanor. 'Why would it?'

Janine took a mouthful and tried to catch up with the conversation. 'What's this?'

'Tina's baby,' Tom said.

Baby! Janine felt the thump in her chest as her heart jumped. She choked on the food, coughing and spitting it

34

out. Eleanor stared at her and Michael turned round to see what was going on but Tom, oblivious, carried on, 'Eleanor thinks it's well good just 'cos Dad said she can babysit. I'm not having it in my room. All babies do is cry.'

'You didn't know?' Michael said, shocked.

'I do now,' Janine said.

'Dad probably didn't get chance to tell you,' Eleanor said.

A baby. How could he? Starting a family with Tina, did he not see how hurtful that would be to Janine? To the kids? As if what he had, two sons, two daughters, was not enough.

Janine's eyes stung and she sniffed hard, cleared her throat.

'He wanted to surprise you,' Tom announced, navigating the strange territory of the grown ups' world.

He's done that, all right, Janine thought. 'Yes,' she smiled at Tom.

'But it won't go in my room, will it Mum?' he said.

'No,' she promised.

The kids barely got enough attention from Pete as it was, a new baby would make it even worse. No wonder he had been so awkward that morning, eager to escape. He was like a child sometimes, pretending that hiding a thing meant everything was all right. Just as Janine had hoped life was getting back onto an even keel, he'd provided her with another huge complicated mess. It felt the same as when Tina and he had shacked up together. Bloody awful.

* * *

The kids were in bed, apart from Michael who was on the computer. Janine stood over Charlotte's cot and watched her sleep. Charlotte sucked her thumb at nights but had relaxed enough now for her to lose the suction and her hand was against her chin, a thoughtful pose. Janine saw the slight movement of the cover as Charlotte breathed, shallow and slow. Being parents was the one thing Janine and Pete shared that Tina wasn't party to. It was special. It had been theirs for the last seventeen years, that and the marriage. It had been a comfort of sorts that although Tina was now Pete's partner, she wasn't the mother of his children. Janine knew she'd get used to it in time, she'd have to, but now she was feeling stupidly jealous and raw.

Her phone rang and she moved out onto the landing and checked the display. If it was Pete she'd not answer. She didn't trust herself to be civil and bawling at him down the phone was not what she wanted to do. Well — she did but it wouldn't achieve anything but cement the hostility that kept flaring up between them. When she read Shap's name, she accepted the call. 'Hello.'

'Boss.'

'Shap, if you're angling for overtime, you can forget it,' she said.

'Clive Wray,' he said, 'Hayfield was hosting a fell race that day. Hundred and forty entrants, stewards and supporters. If he was there, he couldn't have missed it. He said there was no-one much about to alibi him. He's lying to us, boss.'

Janine felt a surge of energy. This was just what they needed to keep the investigation moving forward. She wasn't surprised by the news, people lied a lot, lied to the police as long as they thought they could get away with it. Shap's earlier comments speculating about the family being involved suddenly looked a lot more likely.

CHAPTER 7

Day Two: Tuesday 29 April

Early that morning Janine made her way through the press camped outside the Wrays' house, ignoring the intrusive thrust of cameras and the questions the journalists called out: *Any news for us, ma'am? How are the family coping? What progress have you made? What about the bearded man seen at the park?*

Claire Wray opened the door herself and flinched at the barrage of activity outside.

'Is there any news?' Claire said as they went into the kitchen.

'No, I'm sorry. Is Clive here, Claire?'

'He's out, we've no milk. If you want tea. . .'

'That's fine,' Janine said.

'He won't be long,' Claire said. The woman was so jittery. Her face flickered with emotion, hands busy.

'I need to ask you a very difficult question, Claire. And I wouldn't do so if it wasn't vital,' Janine said.

Claire Wray nodded stiffly, stuffed her hands in her pockets. She looked at Janine directly then away.

'We believe Clive is lying to us about going walking,' said Janine.

'I don't know what to think anymore,' Claire said urgently.

Janine scalp prickled. Claire knew something. 'Claire?'

'The suspicion. It just grows and poisons everything. I thought I was being paranoid. He was so jumpy every time anyone asked us where we were. I thought I was going mad. His boots were clean. I looked in his pockets. I was going to ring you.' Claire pulled a sheet of paper from her pocket. She handed it to Janine along with a little ticket.

'That's where he was,' she said agitatedly. 'Look at the date. He's lying. A time like this and he's lying. Why would he lie, when Sammy . . . why would he lie?' She was distraught, close to breaking down, her eyes wild.

Janine took in the contents of the flyer.

'Thank you. I realise how very difficult this must be and I'll make sure we find out exactly what's going on. Can I ask you to keep this between ourselves for now until I've had time to look into it?'

Claire, her mouth working with worry, nodded.

'There may be a very simple explanation but you did the right thing telling me,' Janine reassured her, when they heard the door opening.

'Mr Wray,' Janine said.

'Hello?' he said. He went to put the container of milk in the fridge.

'I'm afraid I have no news as yet but I wanted to call and see if either of you had anything to add to your statements.'

Clive shook his head, 'No, sorry.'

'Have either of you remembered anything fresh about the day Sammy went missing or the period leading up to it?'

'The vandalism,' Claire said suddenly.

'What?' said Janine.

'We had these incidents, the car was scratched and the tyres let down, then we had a stone thrown at the window,' she said.

'You didn't report this to the missing persons inquiry?' Janine said.

'It was weeks before, it was just kids,' Clive said dismissively. 'You get a spate of things and then it goes quiet.'

'Could you make a note for me,' Janine asked them. 'When the incidents occurred, exactly what happened.'

'You think there might be a connection?' Claire said.

'Just being thorough, we don't know yet what is significant and what isn't but it is important to consider everything.'

Claire nodded, wringing her hands.

As she left them, Janine wondered if Claire had the fortitude to keep quiet about what she had uncovered or whether she would crack under the pressure and confront Clive. The sooner the inquiry could establish exactly what was going on with Clive Wray the better.

* * *

'We know he wasn't hiking,' Janine told Richard as they rode up in the lift to the incident room together. 'But we get the story behind this before we pull him in.' She indicated the leaflet and parking ticket in a protective evidence bag.

Richard's phone rang and he answered, 'Millie.'

He listened and laughed. 'Do you now? Well, you'll have to wait, won't you?'

Oh please, Janine thought. She could do without being party to innuendo-ridden flirting between Richard and Millie. She rolled her eyes at him but he affected not to notice.

'But listen,' he said, 'Clive Wray, his wife's shopped him. He wasn't roaming the dark peak, turns out he was at Sport City.'

Janine bristled. Who was he to go telling the press office what was happening? She was in charge.

'Don't know, yet,' he said.

The lift stopped and the doors opened. There was more dirty laughter from Richard as he ended the call, 'Yeah, catch you then,' and followed Janine out.

Janine glared at him.

'What?' he said.

'I'm the SIO. I decide when and how the press officer is briefed,' she snapped.

Richard looked taken aback. 'She was on the phone. Are you serious?'

Of course she was serious, she wouldn't have bloody-well said it if she wasn't.

'Look,' he said crossly, 'maybe it's a bit tricky for you, Millie and I seeing each other, working the same case together. If that's hard for you to deal with, me dating someone here, if you want me to step down. . .'

God, no! She felt ridiculous, exposed. He was making her out to be some petty bully and implying she was jealous. Besides they had a break in the case, it was all about to escalate. She wanted Richard onside not shipped off to another inquiry.

'It's got nothing to do with that,' she said hotly. 'You're way off the mark.'

'Am I? What then? Enlighten me!'

'I do not have issues about you dating. It's about clear channels of communication, that's all.'

'If you say so.'

'Richard, you can date who you like, it's none of my business.'

'You got that right.'

'As long as it doesn't affect your professionalism,' she said.

He gasped, was about to object but she overrode him. 'Fine, that's sorted. Here.' She passed him the flyer and the parking ticket. 'Get someone onto that. We'll schedule the meeting once we've more information on why on earth Clive Wray was at Sport City.'

'Yes, boss,' he flung the title at her and swung off in the other direction. Was she losing his friendship now along with everything else?

* * *

Shap's trip to the Sport City stadium paid dividends. The place was state of the art. Built to host the Commonwealth Games back in 2002 and now home to Manchester City football team, it included impressive security with comprehensive CCTV coverage. Shap was made comfortable and shown the rudiments of the console so he could view the relevant CCTV footage. The parking ticket was timed for 10.55 and activities had been focused around the playing fields. So he began from that time and concentrated on that location.

Forty minutes later he found film of Clive Wray, Clive being given the bum's rush by a very attractive, young competitor.

'Naughty boy,' Shap murmured and went to see about e-mailing the file across to the inquiry.

Now he sat with the others in the incident room as they all watched the scene: an under-16 girls' hockey match stopped for half-time; a digital time counter on the screen showing 11.45; All Saint's v Marsh High School visible on a scoreboard. Spectators and players milled about as Clive Wray approached a player, a young woman with long dark hair and tried to draw her into a hug. She pushed him away and began shouting at him. Clive Wray appeared to be pleading with her but moved away as people glanced at them.

'Jailbait,' said Shap. 'Not the sort of roving his missus had in mind when she filled his flask.'

Richard said, 'Could explain why he gave us the false alibi.'

'Hang on,' said the boss, 'if you were having an illicit relationship would you be that upfront about it? It couldn't be more public.'

It was obvious to Shap, crystal clear. 'He's shagging her, she's dumped him, he can't take no for an answer. He's just a saddo with a gymslip fixation.'

The boss pulled a face, like she was not convinced at all, and said, 'Bring him in for questioning.'

CHAPTER 8

Janine had made the introductions for the tape and then asked Mr Wray to account for his whereabouts on the day Sammy went missing.

'I've already told you,' he said, 'I drove to Hayfield and—'

'We know you weren't hill-walking,' Janine said crisply. 'At the very least I could charge you with wasting police time.'

'There's no-one can vouch for me, that's all,' Clive Wray said defensively.

Had the man no conscience? 'We can prove you were not where you claimed to be,' Janine said.

'That's ridiculous,' he blustered but she saw the fear in his expression.

Janine indicated that Richard should play the recording. 'DI Mayne is now playing Mr Wray a CCTV recording, item number AS11.'

Clive Wray stared at the laptop screen and Janine saw the blood drain from his face, saw his shoulders sag.

'School finals up at Sport City,' she said.

On the screen the girl was yelling at Clive, he tried to reach her and she moved sharply away. 'Your child went missing and you lied to the people trying to find him. For what? To cover up some seedy affair? Or was it more than that? What else are you lying about?'

'She's my daughter!' he looked at Janine aghast. 'My bloody daughter, Phoebe.' That was the last thing Janine expected though it did answer her doubts as to the public setting for the liaison.

'How dare you imply . . . and then you think I hurt Sammy!'

'You lied to us. You'd better have a very good reason for doing so,' she said coldly. 'I'd like to hear it.'

He heaved a sigh then began to talk. 'When Felicity and I split up, I hoped to still see plenty of Phoebe. That's why we bought the house, it was near enough for her to come round. But Felicity, my ex, she's very volatile, needy.' He shook his head. 'She made our lives hell: coming to the house, abusive calls, turning up at work, threatening to kill herself. All these grand gestures. It was horrendous. In the end, I promised Claire a clean break. But that didn't work either. Felicity just wouldn't let go.' He paused for a moment, biting his lip, then said, 'The very day Sammy was born, Felicity took an overdose, Phoebe had to call an ambulance.'

'When did this all start?'

'I left Felicity when Claire got pregnant,' he said. Janine thought of Pete, how it had been the other way round, leaving her when she got pregnant. Except now. . .

'So you were seeing Claire while you were still married to Felicity?'

'Yes,' he said, jutting his chin forward slightly as if to defend that behaviour but Janine could tell he wasn't proud of it.

'How long had you been seeing each other?'

'Does this matter?' he said bullishly.

'That's for us to decide, not you,' Janine replied.

'Almost two years. Then I left but Felicity kept harassing us until Sammy was about six months old.' His eyes filled with sudden tears and Janine guessed he had remembered afresh why they were here, that his child was missing presumed dead. 'Things calmed down then and recently, well, I felt bad about Phoebe, I wanted to try and see her. I'd been there for the first eleven years and then, the way Felicity was it made it impossible for me to see her. Felicity poisoned her against me. But now she's that bit older, I hoped . . . I thought . . .'

'And the argument at the hockey match?' Richard said.

'I went to watch her play, tried to talk to her. But she's still angry. She told me to piss off.' He gave a shake of the head.

'Where did you go?' said Richard.

'Just drove around, sat in the car.'

'Around where?' said Richard.

'I don't remember,' said Clive Wray.

They persisted for a while trying to get more on his movements but he kept repeating he couldn't recall anything until returning home. True or a fudge?

'Why did you conceal this from us?' Janine said. 'And from the missing persons inquiry?'

'I didn't want to upset Claire,' he replied. 'With Sammy gone and everything. She'd have hated me trying to see Phoebe, I just felt it was too much. And it didn't matter.'

'What matters,' Janine said through gritted teeth, 'is that you have wasted my time and resources and my officers' time while we've been investigating your false account. Time that we could have otherwise spent trying to find out who killed a three-year-old child.'

He swallowed. 'I'm sorry,' he said. 'Do you have to tell Claire?'

'No,' Janine replied, 'but you do.'

* * *

Lies and secrets — the damage they did. Was that really all he'd been lying about?

Janine stood with Richard beside the windows of the incident room watching Clive Wray leave, crossing the tram lines towards Central Library, hunched over against the rain.

'Still no alibi for the afternoon,' Richard said.

'Still no motive,' said Janine.

'Maybe he thought he'd made the wrong choice, that the argument with Phoebe brought it home. Perhaps he felt Sammy was an obstacle?'

'If he wanted to go back to Felicity,' Janine said, 'he could have just upped sticks and gone, he wouldn't need to kill his son. Let's talk to the girl.'

* * *

Felicity Wray's house reeked of incense. Mobiles and wind charms hung from every available place. Batik throws and Indian cottons threaded with gold and silver thread served as coverings for the furniture and curtains in the living room. But the chilled out vibe had little apparent effect on the woman herself, Janine swiftly realised. Felicity Wray seemed close to hysterical, nervy and melodramatic with a latent hostility that simmered behind her words. She swished about in a maxi dress, her arms adorned with bangles and love-beads around her neck, smoking a small cheroot.

Phoebe, a dark-haired 14 year-old was a typical young teen, a mix of innocence and cynicism. Switching between disaffection and naivety within a few sentences. They were trying to talk to Phoebe, who was perched, arms firmly crossed, on the end of a huge sofa, but Felicity kept interrupting.

'Clive says he wanted to try and make contact again,' Janine said.

'He thought he could just say sorry and make it all better. Like — hello?' Phoebe was trying for disaffected teenager but Janine sensed a fragility behind the act.

'That's why you rowed?' Janine said.

Phoebe indicated it was.

'You knew about this argument?' Janine asked Felicity.

'I told her,' Phoebe said.

'She stopped eating, you know, when he left,' Felicity tossed her head, her earrings jingled. 'Starved herse—'

'Mum!' Phoebe blushed furiously. At least Pete still saw his kids, Janine thought. How much harder would it have been if he'd abandoned them? She pictured Eleanor, 11 now and the same age as Phoebe was when Clive left. Eleanor would be completely crushed by something like that.

'It's the truth,' Felicity said to her daughter. 'And your schoolwork suffered, he never thought about that, did he?'

'Mum, don't,' Phoebe muttered.

This was impossible. Janine nodded to Richard signalling with her eyes that he should concentrate on Felicity. Janine moved around the other side of the sofa, putting herself in between mother and daughter.

'Was it a difficult break up?' Richard asked Felicity.

'Had he tried to see you before?' Janine said to Phoebe.

But Phoebe didn't reply, she seemed intent on listening to what her mother was telling Richard. 'He made such a mistake, abandoning us. I think he knows that now. Clive and I, a love that deep — it's not a bond you can ever break. If it hadn't have been for the baby—'

'Mum!' Phoebe said. Janine saw she was trying to protect her mother.

'Phoebe?' Janine said, 'Your dad, he'd not contacted you before?'

The girl, shook her head rapidly. 'No. Well, he came round here with Sammy a few weeks ago. Some deranged plan that if we got to know him it'd change everything. *Soo* not a good idea,' she said.

Something else Clive Wray had failed to mention. Did he think they were idiots, that this wouldn't come to light, just like his trip to see Phoebe at the stadium had done?

Felicity was still waxing lyrical. 'He'd never have left me but for that. He wants us back. He's just in denial.'

Janine saw a spasm of irritation on the girl's face as she swivelled round on the sofa arm and said hotly, 'We're second best. He picked Claire, he picked Sammy.' Janine knew the feeling. Pete had picked Tina. How much more painful if a child had been involved then? Janine sensed the loneliness, the rejection that the girl felt. It was all so keen at that age, so cut and dried.

Phoebe jumped to her feet. 'When Mum was ill, she,' Phoebe hesitated, flushed, 'she took an overdose. I had to stay at Dad's. I was invisible. My mum had nearly died but all they could think about was Sammy. Dad didn't want me there and she didn't. They just wanted to live happily ever after—' her voice was cracking.

'It must have been hard,' Janine said.

Phoebe blinked back tears but didn't say anything.

'You met Sammy?' Richard said to Felicity.

She stared at him, Janine could see a smirk twitching at the corners of her mouth. She took a drag on the cheroot. 'I never wished the child any harm.'

'Mum—' Phoebe tried again to stop her talking but Felicity was apparently determined to say her piece, 'I just wished it hadn't been born.' She looked at Janine then Richard. 'You think that's a terrible thing to say?'

'He's only little,' Phoebe looked upset. 'It's not his fault.' She sat down heavily. 'How could anyone do that?'

Felicity moved over and put a hand on Phoebe's head. 'I know,' she murmured. 'Poor Claire.' Her tone hollow, disingenuous. She didn't mean a word of it.

'I've got hockey practice,' Phoebe announced.

Janine looked at Richard, he'd no objection. They had got what they had come for, for now, corroboration of Clive's relationship with Phoebe and the context for their meeting. They'd also found someone else who was worth considering, Janine thought, Felicity Wray the wronged ex-wife with an axe to grind.

'Bunny boiler,' Richard said as they reached the car outside the house.

'A credible suspect?' Janine asked.

'Certainly got motive, revenge,' Richard said.

'Felicity hates Clive for destroying the marriage,' Janine agreed.

'But she wants him back,' Richard said. 'She blames Sammy for Clive leaving. Maybe seeing the child triggers that rage. She thinks with Sammy out the way, Clive'll come back to her.'

'Helluva grand gesture. Mind you, fond of those,' said Janine. 'The suicide attempt on the day Claire goes into labour.' Janine tried to imagine herself doing something like that to queer the pitch for Tina, and failed.

Richard said, 'Or the girl? Angry, jealous. You saw how she was shielding her mother.'

'Phoebe does it for Felicity?' Janine said.

'Or for herself?'

'Children who kill — they're invariably very damaged. I didn't get that impression, she was upset, maybe confused but nothing extraordinary given the situation.'

'Living with Felicity can't have done her much good,' Richard said. 'Must have messed her head up.'

Janine considered it. She couldn't see Phoebe abducting and then killing her half-brother. But Felicity? 'The witnesses from the park — they say there was a woman there on her own. Could it have been Felicity or Phoebe? Make that a priority tomorrow.'

CHAPTER 9

He came back.

Claire's first instinct when she heard Clive's key in the door was to hide. To run upstairs and climb into the fitted wardrobe, like Sammy used to, or wriggle under their bed.

Instead she forced herself to stay where she was at the kitchen table, which was littered with bits of the kitchen roll she had been shredding. Tearing the sheets into smaller and smaller strips.

Did he know she had told police about his boots? Given them the flyer?

Here he was, back home, so the police must have had some answers to their questions or they'd have kept him longer, wouldn't they?

He stood in the doorway, almost as if he needed permission to cross the threshold. His face sombre.

She raised her eyes to meet his, a bite of fury piercing the numbness that kept descending on her. His eyes told her nothing.

'What happened?' she said.

He cleared his throat, 'They wanted to know where I was.' He moved into the room, pulled off his jacket, displacing the

49

air and sending pieces of kitchen roll fluttering on to the floor. He sat opposite her.

'I'm, erm . . . Hayfield . . . I wasn't at Hayfield.' He tapped his right thumb and index finger together, nervously.

She waited, unwilling to supply questions, to ease his admission.

'I should have told you, I know that now.'

He was having an affair! Oh God. What a fool she had been. She should have seen it coming. He'd left Felicity for Claire and now he was leaving Claire for whoever was next in line. While she had been running round the park frantic for her son, dread thickening her blood, Clive had been screwing some woman.

He swallowed, made to speak and failed. Claire picked up some shreds of paper began to roll them in her fingertips into a little ball.

'It was . . . I was seeing Phoebe,' he said.

Phoebe. The other woman is called Phoebe?

'She was playing in the schools' hockey tournament at the stadium.'

Claire looked at him, his wretched face. 'Your Phoebe?' she said.

'I know we'd agreed to keep a distance, that with Felicity poisoning her towards us it was the only way but I felt . . . I thought . . . Now she's that bit older.'

She felt a wave of anger crash through her. 'Why didn't you tell me?'

'Because I'd promised you not to have anything to do with them, because when Sammy was gone it didn't seem to matter. All that mattered was getting Sammy back. How could I upset you more by—'

'Upset me? Oh, for pity's sake, Clive, I was deranged already. I couldn't have cared less about you and your cosy father-daughter date.'

'It wasn't exactly like that,' he muttered.

'I don't care,' she snapped. 'What I do care about is that you lied. To me.' She was on her feet.

'Of course.' His eyes fell. 'Look, I'm sorry I misjudged—'

'Misjudged!' Had he really so little idea? 'I thought, God, I even thought . . .' she still couldn't say it.

'What? Claire, please?'

'I thought there could only be one reason someone would lie to the police like that.' Tension sang in the air and his eyes filled with horror as he grasped what she meant and cried out, 'No, you can't possibly—'

'I did. Thanks to you. I couldn't trust you anymore. Because of that stupid lie.'

'You knew? But how?' he said. So the police had not told him what she had discovered.

'Does it matter?'

'And you thought I—' His temper broke then, 'How dare you?' he shouted. 'I love Sammy, I love him every bit as much as you and I would never ever . . .' he sputtered to a halt. 'How could you think that? OK I lied about where I was but to imagine . . . to jump to that conclusion. That I might—'

'What else was I supposed to think?' she screamed. 'You lied. Sammy was gone. Probably lying dead already in that drain and you couldn't tell the truth. If I couldn't trust you to be honest then, what hope is there?'

He didn't answer.

She could not tolerate being in the same space as him. She walked slowly away, too drained to cry anymore.

CHAPTER 10

Janine had sent Butchers and Shap to talk to those witnesses who'd seen a woman on her own at the park when Sammy was taken. Richard was updating the incident board with the new details about Clive Wray and his first family and other information from the various lines of inquiry. Janine was in her office catching up on reports from the different teams and trying to plan a strategy for the next twenty-four hours when Millie came in.

'I've just had The Star on. Donny McEvoy's trying to flog them pictures from the crime scene. Took them with his phone.'

Janine groaned. 'What a prat,' she said, 'they're not biting?'

'No. They know the score,' Millie said.

Richard interrupted them. 'A witness sighting of a woman hanging outside the Wrays' on Foley Road on Saturday the nineteenth of April. "Hippie—chick,"' Richard quoted, '"but a bit past it. Frizzy blonde hair."'

'Felicity Wray,' Janine said. 'Why didn't this come up in the missing persons inquiry?'

'The girl who reported it was visiting her father, went home on the Sunday morning, so they missed her on the first door-to-door,' he said.

'Let's see what Mystic Meg has to say for herself?' she invited him.

* * *

'Phoebe's not here,' Felicity Wray said when she answered the door.

'It's you we want to talk to,' Richard told her.

'Honoured I'm sure,' she said archly, turning away and leaving them to follow her in.

'Saturday the nineteenth of April, you were seen at Foley Road, shortly before one pm.'

'Was I?' she said with that little smirk.

'What were you doing there?' said Richard.

'If Clive wants to play daddy to Phoebe again then he'll have to give it one hundred percent, I went to tell him that.'

'You want him to come back to you?' Janine said.

'Yes. I went to tell him. All or nothing. When I think what he'd done. Our lovely girl, he abandoned her, cut her dead. He almost destroyed me. I know what it means to be insane with grief.'

Oh, please, spare me.

'You knew Clive had been up to see Phoebe playing in the tournament?'

'Yes, she rang me on her way home — so upset.'

'And what did Clive say?' Richard asked.

'Oh, he wasn't there, no-one in,' Felicity said.

'So you went to the park?' Janine said. 'You saw Sammy and Claire.'

Felicity ignored her. She stroked her neck, speaking dreamily. 'He loves me. That's what people miss. That connection, the passion—'

Janine interrupted her, 'They looked happy, Claire and Sammy. You and Phoebe had been happy, you and Phoebe and Clive. Until Sammy came along.'

'Times like this, people see what really matters,' Felicity said. 'Like Clive and I. It'll bring us closer in the end.'

The self-obsession of the woman. Janine lost patience. 'Did you go to the park?' she demanded.

Felicity surveyed her for a moment, one eyebrow raised. 'You're holding on to a great deal of anger.'

Janine felt heat in her face.

'Mrs Wray,' Richard said in warning.

'No,' Felicity said.

'And after that?' Janine said.

'Had a walk, came home.'

'And Phoebe?' Richard said.

'She was here.'

'What time was that?' he said.

'I don't wear a watch,' she said.

'Mrs Wray do you know anything about the abduction of Sammy Wray?' Janine said curtly.

'Only what I've seen on the news,' she replied.

'We may well want to speak to you again,' Janine said.

'Well, I won't leave town, then,' Felicity Wray said.

Janine left the room before she lost all reason and clocked her one.

'She's messing with us,' she said to Richard once they got into the car. 'I think if she was involved, she'd tone it down a bit, don't you?'

'If she was at the park and wearing that get-up then wouldn't the witnesses have mentioned it?' Richard said.

'You know eyewitnesses — notoriously unreliable. We'll see what Shap and Butchers have found out,' Janine said. 'But we need to get to the bottom of this happy family's malarkey and eliminate Looby Loo in there, and Phoebe and Clive Wray or look a lot deeper. Why didn't Clive tell us he'd taken Sammy round there? Maybe that's what kick-started this whole bloody mess.'

'Maybe that's what he's afraid of,' Richard said.

'Let's ask him.'

* * *

54

It was a very fine line to tread. Claire and Clive could well be bereaved parents and nothing more. If the Wray household had an air of tension on Janine's previous visit it was now stretched to breaking point.

Claire wore the same clothes as the previous day. Had she even slept, Janine wondered. Sue, the family liaison officer, looked tired too and when Janine asked her how everyone was, she gave a look of warning.

Clive and Claire Wray were at opposite sides of the room, Claire in the corner of the sofa, gazing at the floor, Clive standing over by the window.

'We've been speaking to Felicity, Mr Wray.'

He stilled and Janine saw Claire look up. 'Why did you take Sammy to see her?' Janine said.

Claire Wray gasped, her mouth open with shock.

'He's just a little boy,' Clive Wray said, 'she acted as if he was the devil incarnate . . . I just thought if she saw him, got to know him—'

Claire stood up quickly, stumbled a little. 'You took our son to see that bloody woman — after everything she did to us—' She stopped abruptly, her frown clearing as if she'd made a discovery. 'The car, the tyres and the scratches. That was her again, wasn't it? Not vandals.' A reprise of the harassment that Felicity had subjected the couple to when Clive first left.

He began to object but Claire raised her voice. 'You still love her, don't you? Felicity's been right all along. You only left her because I was pregnant. You never really loved me. Always Felicity, wasn't it?'

'No,' Clive Wray said.

'Bloody tragic Felicity and her precious daughter,' she was shouting, spittle flying from her mouth, her face suffused with red. 'She couldn't even let me give birth in peace — had to grab the spotlight, try and kill herself.'

'Claire, please,' Janine made an effort to calm the situation.

Claire glared at her then her face changed and she visibly crumpled, 'My boy,' she said quietly.

'She'd never touch him,' Clive said insistently.

'How do you know that? How can you possibly know that? She's off her head and you let her meddle in our lives whenever she likes.'

He turned to Richard, 'You've no reason to think so,' he appealed.

Richard took a breath. 'Felicity was seen outside this house, on the nineteenth; she admits she came here.'

'She killed him,' Claire said in horror. 'It's your fault. That mad bitch came and took him. See what you've done,' she was sobbing, frantic with grief. Then she lunged at her husband, screaming. Richard and Sue moved in to separate the couple. Janine called out to Claire to calm down. Claire was slapping at Clive's head. He tried to dodge the blows. Sue got hold of Claire's shoulders and as she eased her back, Richard stepped in between the couple.

At that moment Janine's phone rang. She stepped back to take the call. She asked them to repeat the information and then she said, 'Are you sure? There's no doubt whatsoever?' She felt the blood drain from her face.

Clive Wray was shouting back now, 'Felicity is not a killer. And I love you, Claire. You and Sammy and Phoebe. I may have lost one child but I'll fight damn hard now to be a father to the other one.'

Janine put her phone away. Clive was still talking, Claire shivering as he said. 'I can't have Sammy back but I still want a life with you — and I want my daughter in it. That's how it'll be. And if you love me, you'll accept that.'

Richard saw Janine's expression and saw that something had shifted. Something had happened.

'What?' he said.

She took a breath and moved closer. 'Clive, Claire.'

They looked at her. Claire distraught, dishevelled and Clive breathless.

'Oh, I am so sorry,' Janine said. 'The child, the little boy we found. It's not Sammy. They've got the DNA results back. It's not Sammy.'

It was as if the air had been sucked from the room. A moment where no-one moved and then all hell let loose. Claire flew at Janine, hitting out at her and crying. Clive began shouting, 'What do you mean? Where's Sammy? You said—'

Janine pulled Claire close, so she couldn't keep thumping her, and held her while she wept.

CHAPTER 11

Detective Superintendent Louise Hogg never raised her voice, didn't need to, but the message was crystal clear to Janine in every crisp syllable. The two women were in Hogg's office and Janine was acutely aware that her team out in the incident room, could see through the glass partition that she was receiving a comprehensive bollocking.

'So, Sammy Wray is still missing plus you have no idea who the murder victim is. You've lost two days following false trails for the murder, two days acting as though the abduction led to it.'

'We never said it was Sammy Wray,' Janine pointed out.

'But you assumed it was, you let that determine your strategy, your actions,' Louise Hogg said.

'The same age, sex, colouring, they had the same t-shirt,' Janine tried to defend herself.

'The most popular high street range, as I recall. The Chief Constable is waiting to hear from me. He wants to know exactly how we're helping Sammy's parents, how we intend to reassure the community and how we'll protect the force's reputation. What can I tell him?' She stared at Janine, displeasure clear in the set of her expression.

Janine cleared her throat, stood up straighter. 'That no-one is more dedicated to solving this than me and my team. That we will pursue every possible line of inquiry, and that I have no doubts of our eventual success.'

'All very well, but what we need is a breakthrough. Instead we've been stuck down a blind alley for forty-eight hours.'

Louise Hogg gave a curt nod of dismissal and Janine left, feeling awful.

The team were studiously avoiding eye contact with her, pretending to be occupied as she made her way through the incident room to her own office. Would she lose their trust, their support because of this?

'Tea, boss?' Lisa spoke up and Janine felt a moment's gratitude towards the young DC.

'Ta, no — make it coffee. Then separate all the data on the boards out, everyone else the same with your reports, divide them into those related to the abduction and those relating to the murder. Meeting in an hour-and-a-half, anyone out in the field call them in.'

Murmurs of assent rippled round the room. Perhaps it was too early to say but she didn't feel any air of resentment. Maybe they were all as surprised as she had been at the shock revelation. And as gutted.

* * *

Her preparation wasn't as thorough as she would have liked for the new briefing, disentangling the evidence and information of the Sammy Wray disappearance from that of the murder was complicated but Janine felt it was more important to give the team some sense of momentum, to reinvigorate them rather than have all the details finessed and neatly presented.

Once everyone was in the room, including Millie, Louise Hogg joined them, no doubt putting in an appearance to indicate she thought Janine required close supervision. Janine felt as though she had been caught out, found wanting. It wasn't a sensation she liked. Was she losing her touch? Was there anything she could have done differently? Would another SIO have handled things any better? It was a genuine mistake, assuming the body was Sammy Wray, everything had seemed to point that way.

Now she had to hold it together, give a lead, no matter how badly shaken she was by the turn of events.

Two distinct investigation boards had been established. The one on the left read Murder, it held all the details from the crime scene, information on individuals linked to the location: the builders, the Staffords and the Palfreys, other neighbours. The post-mortem summary was there, as were forensics from the scene.

The board on the right was headed Missing Person: Sammy Wray. Sammy's photo was there, details about the Wrays and Felicity and Phoebe, information from the park inquiry, including the references to the single woman, elderly couple and the bearded man.

Each board now had its own distinct timeline.

Janine began, 'We have an abduction and we also have the murder of an unknown child. A week last Saturday, three-year-old Sammy Wray was abducted from Withington Park. Two days ago, the body of a child was recovered from Kendal Avenue, a mile away. This child was of similar age and appearance, but he is not Sammy Wray. Sammy Wray is officially a missing person again. Sammy's been gone eleven days now. We will discuss that case first. Sammy's father Clive Wray lied to us about his whereabouts and still has no alibi for the time of the abduction. Mr Wray claims he was driving around in his car after an argument with his daughter Phoebe and can't remember where he was. He also failed to mention that he had taken Sammy to visit his ex-wife Felicity Wray without Claire's knowledge. A neighbour reports seeing a woman matching Felicity Wray's description outside Clive's house on the Saturday afternoon. Felicity Wray denies going to the park but we are trying to establish whether the single woman from eye-witness reports is her. Latest on that?' Janine looked to Shap and Butchers.

'Three witnesses, all agree the woman had long hair, two say blonde, one says brown. Age varies between twenty-five and forty,' Shap said.

'Could do a line-up — see if people identify Felicity as the single woman at the park?' Richard suggested.

Janine nodded. 'Phoebe's another contender for that. We talk to her, too. Her mother says she was at home but I'm not sure we can take her word for it. Felicity Wray has made no effort to hide her resentment of the missing child or her belief that Clive Wray belongs with her and Phoebe. She has a stronger motive then Clive, so she is at present our key candidate.'

'Did you search her house?' Louise Hogg said.

Christ! What if Sammy was there? Been there all along. Alive? Dead? Did they have enough grounds? Louise Hogg obviously thought so. 'We'll get a warrant,' Janine said decisively, 'bring her in for further questioning as well as the line up. And,' she took a breath, 'look into her recent harassment of Clive and Claire — what threats has she been making? Where are we up to with tracing other witnesses?'

'We've found the older couple from the park,' Lisa said. 'They were visiting a relative in hospital.'

'The weirdy beardy man?' Janine said.

'Nothing,' Lisa said.

'Other actions?' Janine surveyed the room, inviting contributions. The team needed to be involved, invested in the case not simply told what to do.

'Revisit the sex offenders, anyone suddenly gone underground and so on,' said Shap.

Janine nodded.

'And if you rule out Felicity Wray?' Louise Hogg said.

'The cases could still be linked,' Richard said, 'someone targeting three-year-olds.'

'Or there could be no connection. We deal with these as two distinct inquiries,' Janine said. If a connection did emerge then so be it but until then the investigations would be treated as distinct and discrete.

'Reconstruction for the abduction set for one pm tomorrow,' Millie said, 'and Press Release in hand informing the media of the new situation.'

'We don't want scaremongering, hysteria,' Janine said to Millie, though she felt close to hysteria herself, panic and confusion inside. 'We need to reassure people.'

'Damage limitation,' said Millie, 'that's all I can try to do. Journalists are asking the same questions we are: is it a series, is Sammy still alive? If I can't give them anything they still have front pages to fill, they've got their own agenda.'

'Selling papers,' Janine said.

'It's a huge story,' Millie explained, 'doesn't get much bigger.'

No doubt there would be negative opinions expressed in the media about the conflation of the two inquiries but Janine felt the best way to handle criticism was head on, to be visible rather than hide away. 'I'll attend the reconstruction,' she said.

Janine moved to the other board. 'Child murder, this is not Sammy Wray, so who is it? We have as you know no recent reports of other missing children of that age in the country. One case in London, three-year-old boy, is a suspected kidnapping as a result of a custody battle but that child was only taken four days ago. Our victim has been dead for longer. Interpol have identified several missing children. So far the only one of particular interest, of the right age and gender and similar physical description is Tomas Rink.' She indicated the photograph of the child. 'We have requested a DNA comparison.' If it was Tomas Rink, how had he ended up in a sewer in South Manchester? Trafficking was a possible explanation, there was an abhorrent and lucrative market in selling children to paedophiles and pornographers, though their child had not borne any obvious signs of sexual abuse. 'With no ID for the child, we concentrate on the site.'

She heard a sharp intake of breath and wheeled round.

'Boss,' Shap pointed to the television, on but muted, in the corner, 'McEvoy.'

Janine saw the builder expounding to some news camera.

'I thought we'd sorted this,' she said to Millie.

'So did I,' Millie said sharply.

'What's he saying? Turn it up,' said Janine.

Lisa hit the remote and McEvoy's Scouse twang, filled the room. 'I've seen some things in my time but that ... wrapped in a sheet but you could tell it was a body. He'd been there a while and I'd been working just a few yards away. Beggars belief.'

'Turn it off,' Janine snapped. 'I want him gagged. Talk to him,' she said to Shap. It was crucial to stop Donny McEvoy from speaking to the press, his meddling could seriously hamper the investigation not only because it might directly influence public attention in the wrong way but even more importantly it could be held up as prejudicial if the case made it to trial 'Why's he so keen?' she said.

'Most exciting thing that's ever happened to him,' Richard said.

'Or did he have a hand in it? Who else apart from the builders had easy access to the site?'

'The property developer is on a lounger in Mexico,' said Lisa.

'Verify that,' Janine said.

'Neighbours,' said Butchers, 'the Palfreys and the Staffords. Staffords couldn't get rid of us quick enough.'

'Wouldn't be that hard for anyone to access,' Richard pointed out. 'No gates on the drive, might still be just a matter of convenience.'

'Well, we eliminate them all before we take this any wider. Record checks, background checks. Be thorough. We have ruled out the house at 16 Kendal Avenue as the primary crime scene?'

'That's right,' Richard said, 'no evidence the child had ever been inside the property.'

So many questions. Who was the child? Where had he come from? Where had he been killed? 'We're starting afresh with this,' she said. 'Look at everything as though it's completely new to you. We've two crimes here. Two boys. We need to find one of them. And identify the other.'

CHAPTER 12

Janine was gathering papers together in preparation for the interview with Felicity. Richard came in and handed her a card to sign, for Butcher's engagement.

'If that child was there when we went round . . .' Janine looked at him.

Richard shook his head. 'No word yet.'

She couldn't think of anything more original than 'Good Luck' to put in the card, she scrawled her name beneath it.

'Butchers has put his 'do' back an hour. You going?' Richard said.

'Doubt it. Need to get my head round this lot. You?' She passed him the card.

'Show my face,' Richard said.

'Taking Millie?'

'Might be,' he said.

Why did he have to be so bloody coy about it? 'Only asking,' she retorted, sounding more defensive than she'd intended.

Half-an-hour later he was back, 'Felicity Wray's in interview room one.'

'Thanks,' said Janine getting to her feet.

'We got the data of the texts that she sent Clive Wray,' Richard said, 'nasty stuff.'

'He didn't delete them?'

'Maybe he wanted some proof in case anything weird happened,' he said.

'Like child abduction?' she said.

* * *

By the time Janine started the interview proper after making introductions for the tape, Mrs Wray had already made her displeasure clear, sighing and shuffling in her seat, twirling her hair around her fingers. Even yawning.

'You've been up to your old tricks, Mrs Wray. Attacking property, threatening Clive and his family,' Janine said.

'Second family,' Felicity said.

'We've read some of the messages you sent him,' Janine picked up the transcript and quoted, '"Your life won't be worth living. Your slut and her brat can rot in hell." This all started up again after he brought Sammy round.'

'What did he expect? Rubbing my face in it. He knew I resented that child,' she said.

'Resented, past tense?' Janine said.

'You think he's still alive?' Felicity said.

'Do you know any different?' Janine said seriously. It was hard to believe the woman was still being so cavalier.

'She put you up to this, didn't she? Trying to blame me. She was the one that lost the child. She took Clive and now she's still persecuting me. She knows where Clive really belongs, that's why.'

Janine refused to be drawn.

'You are aware that we are searching your property?' Janine said, 'Is there anything you'd like to tell me about, anything we might find?'

Felicity Wray gave a little shake of her head, 'Only that it seems to be a dreadful waste of police resources.'

Felicity Wray maintained her big show of finding the questions tiresome but Janine felt she enjoyed the attention, a chance to perform as the wronged woman, the victim in her very own soap opera.

Was she just a narcissist, interested only in her own tribulations, indifferent to the fate of a small child or the hell that the supposed love of her life was going through? Or was this self-obsession of a much darker nature? Jealousy led people to commit terrible acts.

'I'd like to ask you again, did you enter Withington Park on the nineteenth of April?'

'No.'

'Did you take Sammy?'

Felicity Wray rolled her eyes. 'No.'

'Do you know where he is?'

'No.'

'We are entering your details into a video identification parade to see if any witnesses at the park remember seeing you there.'

Felicity Wray shrugged. 'Knock yourselves out,' she said.

* * *

'What do you think?' Richard asked her as they waited in her office while the video parade was carried out.

Janine raised her hands, palms up. *Search me.* Nothing untoward had been found at Felicity Wray's house, so far. A more detailed examination of the premises was still in progress.

'She's cracked enough,' Richard said.

'Let's see what we get out of the line-up,' Janine said.

Millie Saunders came through the incident room, and knocked on Janine's door.

'Yes,' Janine said.

There was a look of exasperation on Millie's face. 'My phone's in meltdown. Local press has got wind of an arrest. Half of them are camped outside. Is it true you're questioning the ex-wife for the abduction?'

'We are,' said Janine.

'Thanks for the update,' Millie said sarcastically.

'We have been rather busy,' Janine said.

'I should be told of all major developments,' Millie said. 'This is a major development?'

At exactly the same moment as Janine answered no, Richard said yes.

* * *

Millie shook her head in disgust, gave a humourless laugh. 'Final answer?' she said.

'There's a lot of speculation flying about at this stage,' Janine said.

'Well, unless you give me something to work with, that speculation is going to be all over the airwaves as well. Or shall I put the calls through to the incident room? To the horse's mouth?'

For one delirious moment Janine considered telling Millie Saunders to bugger off. Instead she took a steadying breath and then said coolly to Richard, 'Please brief Millie, make sure she's up to speed on all developments. Now, and for the duration of the investigation.' She held her hand out towards the door, inviting them to leave. 'And Richard — no names to be released yet.'

You think he's still alive? Felicity Wray had taunted her. It wasn't likely. Though it depended on who had taken him, or more specifically what for. Janine's gut instincts told her that while Felicity Wray had some motive to want the child out of the picture, she was an unlikely kidnapper. The way she made no attempt to hide her dislike of Clive's new family, her jealousy, also suggested her innocence. If she actually had taken Sammy surely she would be more circumspect and not go all out to antagonise the police. However if a lone paedophile was behind the abduction he might well have got rid of Sammy Wray within the first few hours after abusing him. Rape and murder. A ring of paedophiles would trade the boy as long as they could get away with it, keeping him enslaved for years. It didn't bear thinking about — except for the fact that it was Janine's job to think about such horrors, to face them squarely and calmly, analytically, to examine the evidence and try and reach the truth. Her colleagues at CEOPS who concentrated solely on child exploitation and protection had been alerted.

Janine's phone went — Lisa at Felicity Wray's house. They had not found Sammy, nor any trace of him and there was no sign of any attempts to conceal a body, like recent digging in the garden. Thank God. If they had found the child there Janine would never have been able to forgive herself. And neither would Louise Hogg.

CHAPTER 13

Butchers had tolerated the stupid balloons and the noose above his desk as best he could but when he saw Lisa handing cash over to Shap he couldn't let it lie.

'Are you doing a whip-round?' Butchers hissed.

'Who pissed on your chips?' Shap said.

'I told you I didn't want any fuss. It's just a small do,' Butchers said.

'Don't know what you're on about, mate. I'm collecting for the lottery. We're in a syndicate.' Shap was a weaselly bastard, lie his way out of any situation and Butchers didn't know whether to believe him.

Butchers returned to his desk. He had been speaking to the community policing team who covered the Kendal Avenue area, checking out the neighbours and any known criminals. He was particularly interested to learn that Luke Stafford was already on their radar. Anti-social behaviour, police had been called to the school twice to deal with violent incidents.

'Luke Stafford — bit of a bad 'un,' Butchers told Shap. Then he compared his notes and saw something else. 'And, he goes to All Saints — same school as Phoebe Wray.' Fluke or something more sinister? Butchers thought about it: Phoebe Wray is half-sister to the missing boy and Luke Stafford lives next door to where the dead child was found. OK, the boss had stressed the importance of keeping the two inquiries separate but a coincidence like that at the very least needed explaining.

The office phone rang and Shap answered it, listened then said, 'Kim, Tony Shap here — your fiancé's better half.'

Butchers shook his head, raised a warning hand — *I'm not here*. He felt sick. He'd blanked three calls from Kim already. It was busy and he was up to his eyes. If she was mithering him like this now, then just how much worse would it be once they were hitched?

'Just missed him,' Shap said smoothly. 'All systems go for tonight?' He listened and laughed. 'Can't wait.'

Shap hung up and looked to Butchers waiting for an explanation. He could whistle for it. Butchers shrugged, easier than trying to justify his behaviour. Wasn't sure what was going on himself, anyway. No time to be bothering about all that now, he needed to do a bit more digging with Luke Stafford.

Butchers headed for the door then stopped. 'Maybe we should postpone the party — everyone's flat out.'

'No way, mate,' said Shap, 'after the last few days we need a chance to get totally hammered.'

Which was not what Butchers wanted to hear.

* * *

The Staffords' place was still a tip. Didn't look like anyone had picked up anything since Butchers' last visit. Ken Stafford simmered with resentment, if Luke Stafford had a temper, lost control and got into bother, Butchers could tell where he'd got that from. While the father sat in an armchair, sitting forward rather than relaxing back, the lad stood leaning against the door jamb. Butchers had invited him to sit down but the kid had replied, 'Rather stand.'

Butchers started with the Saturday of the abduction. They had already answered questions about that day, he'd lull them into thinking he was just going over the same old ground then chuck something new into the mix. See what it threw up.

'A week last Saturday you were working?' Butchers said to Ken Stafford.

'I told you that,' he said.

'You work nights, so Luke's here on his own?'

'That's right,' Ken Stafford said.

'Then what?'

'We've been over this,' he said.

'I'd like to go over it again,' Butchers said stolidly.

Ken Stafford shifted in his seat, 'Shift finishes at four am,' he said tightly, 'I get in at half past. Slept till five-ish that evening.'

'Long sleep.'

'I needed it,' Ken Stafford retorted. 'I'd only just got off when the bloody builders roll up.'

'You remember this, Luke?' said Butchers

'I was asleep but he told me, later. You never shut up about it,' he complained to his father.

'What time did you get up?' Butchers asked the lad.

'Dunno,' he gave a quick shrug.

'Rest of that day. Where were you?'

'Here, probably,' Luke said.

'You can't remember?'

'Here.'

'And you didn't see Luke for the best part of twenty odd hours?' Butchers said to Ken Stafford.

'That's right,' he said.

'You've been in a bit of bother,' Butchers said to Luke, 'assault, anti-social behaviour. Make you feel big, does it, knocking people about?'

Luke set his jaw, sullen, didn't answer.

Ken Stafford glanced sharply at Butchers.

'You get a buzz out of hurting people?' Butchers said.

'Pack it in,' Ken Stafford threatened Butchers, 'don't talk to him like that.'

'You know Phoebe Wray well?' Butchers asked Luke.

Surprise flashed across the boy's face and he blushed. 'We're mates,' he stammered, 'that's all.'

'Mates,' Butchers echoed. 'She said anything to you about her half-brother's abduction?'

'No,' Luke said.

'Nothing? Odd that.'

'Said you lot went round there.'

'That all?' Butchers said.

'Yeah,' he said. But Butchers had the sense there was more, that Luke was hiding something. He turned to Ken Stafford, 'Have you any objection to me taking a look round?'

'Yes, I have,' Ken Stafford said baldly.

'I could get a warrant,' Butchers said.

'You best do that, then.'

'We normally expect a degree of co-operation in a case involving a child.'

'You get a warrant and we'll co-operate,' the man said. 'And don't come back without one.'

Charm personified.

* * *

Donny McEvoy was having a tea break when Shap caught up with him, mug balanced on a pile of breeze block, rolling tobacco on his knee. 'Mr McEvoy?'

He looked up eagerly, 'You from the papers?' McEvoy's eyes gleamed, the bloke was practically slavering.

Shap flashed his warrant card. McEvoy didn't look quite so keen then.

'My boss,' Shap said, 'she's not very happy. You shooting your mouth off. That could compromise our investigation.'

'I'm only giving my side of the story,' McEvoy protested.

'Not any more, you're not.' Shap lit a fag of his own.

'What about free speech?' McEvoy bleated.

'It isn't free if it costs us the case,' Shap told him. 'Get it? Now — dates, places, times. I need to go over it all with you again.'

'Fine,' he said. 'It's all in here,' he tapped at his head. 'I can see it, that little bundle. It was horrific . . .'

'Back up a-ways,' Shap interrupted. He got out his phone to record McEvoy's answers. 'Let's start at the beginning, how long had you been working at Kendal Avenue?'

* * *

Butchers called Lisa who was at Felicity Wray's to check that the search was still ongoing. It was Phoebe's bedroom he was most interested in and when he walked into it, he could see it looked promising. The posters on the wall were the stuff of nightmares: people in clown masks looking far from funny, blood and gore, vampires and images of war, a band all dressed in skeleton suits. One slogan read, *Death is Freedom*.

He scanned the bookshelves, and then he saw the title: *Children Who Kill* by Carol Anne Davis. He grabbed it and opened the cover. A name written inside, *Luke Stafford*.

'Look at this,' he said to Lisa, 'Luke Stafford has lent her a book on child murders.'

Lisa raised her eyebrows. 'And everyone says kids don't read anymore,' she joked.

Butchers placed the book in a sealed evidence bag. He hadn't pieced it all together yet but there was something here, he could feel it. Two teenagers going off the rails, egging each other on. Impressionable at that age, risk takers, no sense of consequences. Butchers felt a kick of excitement; he was onto them, he was going to hunt them down and bring them in. Not exactly sure who'd done what yet. But both Luke Stafford and Phoebe Wray looked guilty as sin.

CHAPTER 14

Claire's mind was on a loop, *it's not Sammy, it's not Sammy, it's not Sammy*. She found the concept impossible to grasp. The previous forty-eight hours she had been doing her hardest to accept the awful truth; to accept the image of her little boy in a drainage tunnel, his small body lifeless, so terribly damaged they would not let her see him.

She had been carrying that in her heart and now they were telling her that poor child was not her child. They didn't know who he was but they were absolutely certain he was not Sammy.

It was a violent wrench, them snatching away the truth, the certainty, cruel finality, almost as violent as Sammy being stolen in the first place and Claire was reeling from it, unable to reconfigure the features of the dead child into those of a stranger. *It's not Sammy.*

The words didn't sink in. Her body, every fibre from the hair on her skin to the marrow in her bones had been devastated by the shock of Sammy's death, fighting to absorb it. And now to have it reversed, to have this macabre resurrection was incomprehensible. It was so hard to unthink it, unfeel it.

Perhaps he was dead anyway. Was this her mother's instinct recognizing the fundamental truth? That even though this dead child was not her boy, her boy was still a dead child.

She was sick and dizzy with it all. And angry. Angry that suddenly she was expected to readjust. For a third time.

First to be bereft, full of fear and shame, mad with desperation that her boy had gone, disappeared. *Magic, Mummy, Izzy-whizzy.*

Then to be crushed, sobered, broken by the notification of death.

And now, a third yank of the rope, fresh torture.

It hurt when she breathed, her lungs, her ribs were sore.

How dare they, the police, fate, whoever.

The logical part of her brain told her this might yet be a good thing. Sammy might be alive if he's not in that sewer. But her instincts felt heavy, swollen, leaden. Then there were flashes of piercing guilt when she thought that her reprieve meant that somewhere else another mother had lost her son.

Why hope, she thought, so there can be yet another fall? Another blow to the skull, another attack on her heart.

Where was he? Was he frightened? He had a way of freezing, shrinking when he was scared. He wouldn't scream and run, sometimes he didn't even cry, just stilled, frozen like a wary animal.

There were people on the television, voices, news headlines, the police detective — DCI Lewis. Clive turned up the sound.

Claire looked at it stupidly for a second then felt her gorge rise. Sickening. That's what it was. Sickening and brutal and pitiless and she wanted it to stop. All of it. Forever.

CHAPTER 15

Janine was in her office trying to work. Richard and Millie were just outside, Richard looking over the new press release to accompany the reconstruction of Sammy Wray's abduction.

'Great,' Richard said.

'Needs sensitive handling,' Millie said.

'You're good at that,' Richard said with a throaty chuckle.

Oh, please, Janine prayed, enough. It was hard to concentrate without this going on. She got up to close her door and saw Butchers and Lisa arriving back. 'Boss,' Butchers called. Janine went to see what he was so excited about.

'Luke Stafford and Phoebe Wray are mates,' he said. 'He's a history of violent behaviour and he lives next door to the murder scene. She's got reason to want rid of Sammy Wray.'

'What are you saying?' Richard asked before Janine had chance.

'It's a pact,' Butchers answered, 'she does Sammy — he does another child.'

'Oh, come on,' Janine said.

'Or maybe he was going after Sammy, to prove himself to her, like, but he got the wrong child,' said Butchers.

'They're kids,' Janine said incredulously. Murders of children by children were relatively rare. Janine had never worked one in all her years as a detective. When it did happen it sent shock waves through the nation; was held up as evidence of the collapse of society. The names of child murderers lived on for decades in popular imagination: Mary Bell, Jon Venables, Robert Thompson. And as for a pact between a teenage girl and boy, to abduct her half-brother and also to kill another child, it was ridiculous. Butchers was living in some fantasy land.

'You should see her room.' Butchers wasn't giving up, 'Chiller DVDs, stuff about death and pain. Sick stuff. Look,' he waved a book at her, '*Children Who Kill.*'

'I can read,' Janine told him.

'In her room, but it belongs to Luke Stafford. And the stuff all over the walls—'

'She's fourteen,' Janine slapped him down. 'Leonard Cohen, purple ink, crap poetry. I know you sprang fully formed Butchers but the rest of us have been there, got the T-shirts.'

He wasn't deflected. 'The Staffords wouldn't let us look round. They're acting guilty.'

Janine looked to the others for reactions. Were they buying this? Richard shook his head.

But Shap played devil's advocate. 'They're being obstructive. And they are right on the doorstep, plenty of chance to nip out and dump the body.'

'We should interview both Phoebe and Luke,' Butchers said.

Janine considered it for a moment, she didn't agree. 'I know I'm desperate but I'm not that desperate. I'm not pulling juveniles in on the basis of a freaky DVD collection and the fact that they're in spitting distance. Can you put Luke at the park, or Phoebe?' she asked him.

Lisa's phone rang and she answered it.

'Not yet, but I can try,' Butchers glanced at his watch.

'Thought you were otherwise engaged this evening,' Janine said.

Butchers shrugged. Didn't seem particularly buoyant about it.

'Giving her a preview,' Janine said, 'life with a cop?'

Butchers didn't respond, just got a sick look on his face, embarrassed.

'You need a whole lot more than what you're giving me to question either of them,' Janine said.

'Boss,' Lisa held up her phone, she looked fed up. She sighed before she spoke, 'None of the witnesses picked Felicity Wray out of the line-up.'

'Shit,' Janine said succinctly.

They were getting nowhere fast. Nothing at the house, barring Butchers' booty, and now no eyewitness testimony. Janine raised her eyes heavenward and sighed, turned to Lisa and caught sight of Louise Hogg watching from her office. Her old boss Hackett used to do that: snoop and hover, it drove Janine mad. She hoped it wasn't going to become a habit of Hogg's too.

'Release her,' Janine told Lisa. She felt a wave of frustration, almost wanted to weep. The low point of a bloody lousy day. It felt like they were lurching from one false lead to another. First thinking the child was Sammy and now hitting a brick wall with their most likely suspect. When would their luck change? Would it change? Was this going to be one of those cases that ran aground, the sort of case that broke careers, broke people?

She went back to her office and slammed the door, not caring who heard.

* * *

On her way home Janine called to see Claire and Clive Wray. Claire looked empty, her greeting dulled, indifferent. And Clive's reaction on seeing Janine was almost a snarl. The man hummed with suppressed anger. Janine couldn't blame him, even though his duplicity had caused the team problems. She simply could not imagine what it must be like to have believed your child dead and then be informed there'd been a cockup and he was still missing.

'As Sue has told you we've reinstated the missing persons investigation,' Janine said. 'I also wanted to let you know that we have questioned Felicity and released her—'

'You've let her go,' he said quickly.

'We are satisfied that there is no evidence to show she had any involvement.'

'You see,' Clive turned to Claire, 'I told you.'

Claire stared at her husband and gave a short, derisive laugh.

'The reconstruction is timed for one o'clock tomorrow,' Janine said.

'That's it?' Clive Wray demanded, his eyes hot with rage. 'We go through it all for the cameras, so they can plaster it across the news—'

Janine cut him off, 'Yes, that's exactly what we want.' They needed to keep the couple on side, to try and redeem the trust in the police that had been compromised by the mistaken assumptions that Janine and her team had made. The same went for the wider community. If the Wrays made any official complaints or criticised the police to the media the damage would spread.

Momentarily Janine wondered if she should step down, sacrifice herself to try and contain any backlash. Career suicide. But she was not a quitter. She'd be better trying to make things good instead of giving up. 'The right sort of publicity brings us vital information,' she said. 'There are still people we haven't managed to talk to. I'm hoping they'll come forward. But we don't need you to be there, we don't want to make this any harder—'

'Oh, we'll be there,' Clive Wray vowed, 'you can count on that.'

Claire Wray began to speak, not looking at Janine but staring unseeing at the window opposite. 'When you told us that you'd found him, when we believed he was dead, it was so . . . raw and dark. I couldn't breathe,' her voice shook, 'but this — hour after hour wondering — this is worse.'

'I am so sorry,' Janine said. She knew from other cases that the hardest thing for families was often the not knowing, the limbo they were thrust into when people disappeared or when foul play was suspected but no body recovered. Even not knowing how someone had died could haunt those left behind.

'I don't know what's happening to him,' Claire Wray said. 'I watch the clock move, I count his hours. But I'm not there, I should be there.' She began to cry, the tears falling down her cheeks, arms folded across her stomach as she rocked forwards and backwards.

It was Sue who went to comfort her as Clive Wray stood, his fists balled and his face set and Janine forced herself to wait until Claire had stopped weeping to take her leave.

CHAPTER 16

The newspaper headline that greeted Janine when she got home did not help. *Dead Boy Not Sammy. Wray Family Agony.* She threw it across the room then retrieved it. She had to read what they were saying about her, about the investigation, swallow it all, every acidic line and barbed reference.

Tom had been playing up, trying to provoke Eleanor into a fight by calling her names, 'bum face' and 'snot features' among them, snatching more than his share of the apple pie and then refusing to do his homework. Exasperated, Janine had first warned him then banned him from any video games that evening. When he carried on being disruptive she sent him upstairs to cool down for half an hour.

She was on her own in the living room, the telly on, working, when he came back down. She closed her laptop as he wandered into the room.

'Come here,' she said and patted the sofa next to her.

He slumped down and grabbed one of Eleanor's toys, the rag doll which, with a flick of the material, could be changed from Little Red Riding Hood to Granny to the Wolf.

'You OK?' she asked him.

He swung the doll between his hands. 'I don't want Dad to have a stupid baby,' he said.

Me neither.

'Dad will still love you, just the same,' she said, 'like when we had Charlotte. Love doesn't run out — it just stretches.'

'Like an elastic band?' Tom said. He flipped the doll over, bared his teeth at the wolf face.

'Sort of,' Janine said.

'Not for grown—ups, it doesn't,' Tom said, 'like if you get a new wife or a new husband.'

'Ah, no — not then, really. Dad might need a bigger car, though. That won't stretch.'

'Whoa!' Tom said, excited at the prospect.

'And you might like the baby when you get to know it.'

'I won't,' he said solemnly, 'I know I won't.' He yawned.

'Bedtime,' she told him.

It was after ten when she admitted to herself that she wasn't going to get any more done tonight. She'd been staring at the pictures on her laptop for long enough. Claire Wray and Sammy. But she was too tense to go to bed. She was fed up with Pete and strung out about the investigation. And life, even with four kids to cope with, was very lonely sometimes. What she needed was some distraction. A bit of R and R. Then she had an idea. She rang Pete and asked him to come over: something had come up at work.

She went to get changed.

His face when he set eyes on her, in her party gear, was a picture.

'I thought you said work,' he objected.

'Work related,' Janine smiled. 'Tina OK?' she said, giving him a chance to tell her about the baby.

'What? Yeah . . . fine.'

Coward. Why couldn't he just have the guts to be straight with her?

The taxi pulled up then and sounded its horn and she could make a smooth exit without saying something nasty that she'd regret. And without giving him chance to argue the toss about her going out and leaving him to babysit under false pretences.

Good. Be good for the troops as well, she thought *en route*. A bit of solidarity when all eyes are upon us and people are muttering about competence and leadership and judgement.

* * *

How had it come to this? Butchers thought. It was a nightmare. The function room was half empty, a disco blaring out. His mates from the job clustered around the bar, even the Detective Super was here and the boss had just made her appearance. Kim and her gang were ensconced in a corner already totally canned and cackling like demons.

'Next round's on me,' the boss said to them all, then told the bar tender, 'I'll have a double G & T. See what this lot want — and your own.'

Shap nudged Butchers and nodded towards Kim, 'You want to get her name down for *Wife Swap*, mate,' he said, 'she'd be perfect.'

'Piss off,' Butchers told him though he had to admit Kim looked bigger, brassier than he remembered. But their brief courtship had been conducted through a haze of booze, tequila slammers and jagerbombs. The details were hazy.

'So point her out then,' the boss said.

'The one in pink,' Butchers could feel a blush spread through his face.

'Nice,' the boss said. Though it wasn't a word Butchers would have picked.

Detective Superintendent Hogg raised her glass to him. 'Congratulations, Ian.'

'You not speaking then, you and your betrothed?' Shap back on his case, 'Had a tiff already?'

'No,' Butchers said. And then of course he had to go over there and say hello to prove it. What was he meant to do anyway, at a do like this? Sit with Kim or stay with his own guests? Crossing the dance floor as, *I Don't Feel Like Dancing*, by the Scissor Sisters rang out, the phrase *dead man walking* came to mind.

The lasses were gossiping away as he drew closer, people leaning in to catch the dirt and then throwing their heads back in peals of laughter.

'All right?' Butchers nodded to Kim, to the group, as he reached the table and they all cracked up, howling as though he'd delivered a punch line. Feeling a complete twat Butchers wandered back to the bar, a sickly grin on his face and a feeling of dread heavy on his shoulders.

* * *

Janine had got very merry, very quickly and was trying to talk to Richard and Millie above the noise of the bride-to-be and mates belting out a karaoke version of *I Will Survive*. 'Millie,' Janine said, 'we had a tortoise called Millie when I was a kid. Is it short for something? Millicent?'

'Emily, actually,' Millie said and there was a cool tone in her voice.

Just being sociable, Janine thought, no need to take umbrage. 'You don't use Emily for work. Don't you think it'd be a bit more—'

Richard broke in, 'Same again? You do the honours,' he said to Millie.

'Thanks,' Janine passed her glass over.

'I think you've had enough,' Richard said in her ear. *Bloody cheek.*

'Piss off,' Janine told him.

'More what?' Millie said to Janine.

What had they been talking about? Janine had lost track, 'Sorry?'

Millie rolled her eyes.

'So, how long have you two been an item?' Janine tried again. 'He acts like it's a trade secret,' she said to Millie, 'not a married woman, are you?'

'God, no,' Millie said rudely. 'Are you?' Before Janine could respond she'd waltzed off to the bar.

Richard glared at Janine.

'What?' she said.

'Stop stirring it,' he said.

'I'm not,' Janine said.

'Maybe you should call it a night, before you make a fool of yourself,' he said. And he left her there and went after Millie. Janine's cheeks burned, she felt hurt and then angry and then decided to have another drink and sod the lot of them.

* * *

Butchers looked pigsick, Shap noticed. His intended was strutting her stuff with her pals and some lads from uniform, Kim's cleavage on full show.

'You want to nip that in the bud, sharpish,' Shap said nodding at the woman.

Butchers shrugged, 'Not bothered.'

'Not bothered? Her flashing her heirlooms at all comers.'

Another shrug.

'So why did you pop the question?' Shap said, 'Were you pissed?'

'I don't remember. It were news to me. Bad news,' Butchers said.

'You went ahead and stumped up for the ring, though,' Shap said.

Butchers grimaced.

'You tight git,' Shap said. 'You made her buy her own ring? You are kidding me.'

'Just till my salary comes through,' Butchers said, then he added, 'What'm I gonna do?' He reddened, looked ever more awkward, scratched at the back of his neck.

'Leave it to me, mate. I'll have a word,' Shap said.

'Tony,' Butchers protested but it was half-hearted.

'It's sorted. Trust me,' Shap said.

Kim's transformation was instantaneous. From gaudy good-time girl to mouthy harridan as soon as she cottoned on to what Shap was saying, 'Butchers — Ian — he's made a bit of a mistake. When he proposed, it was a bit of a joke, yeah, joke that got out of hand. He wants out. No point in ruining both your lives, eh?'

Eyes glinting, mouth set, Kim cursed like a sailor and scanned the room. Soon as she found Butchers she launched herself in his direction. Her friends, confused but sensing some excitement, followed in her wake.

Shap watched as Kim laid into Butchers with her handbag, smacking him about the head and damning him to hell and back. Assaulting a police officer was an offence under any other circumstances but given the situation who could blame her? Shap didn't reckon anyone was about to slap her in handcuffs.

Over by the bar the boss looked like she was still on a roll. She had been flashing the cash and buying them all drinks and packing a fair few away herself. Now she was flinging her arms around and Detective Superintendent Hogg was concentrating on her rather than the Butchers bust up. Then at that precise moment Hogg looked over to the dance floor and an expression of disgust and resignation rolled across her face. Lady Muck. That's how Shap thought of her and here she was seeing the plebs at play and not enjoying it one little bit. Shap hadn't liked the way Hogg dealt with the boss about the confusion in the identity of the dead child. A genuine mistake that, they'd all expected it to be Sammy Wray, yet Lady Muck behaved as though the boss had done something really brainless. Had given her a right bollocking. Never raised her voice but you could tell from the body language.

Kim had drawn blood, a cut visible on Butchers' face and her friends were getting nowhere fast trying to pull her off, so Shap reckoned he'd better lend a hand before anyone else got hurt.

* * *

'I never took you for a party animal,' Louise Hogg said.

'Live it large, Louise, that's what I say. Show 'em we're human,' Janine said.

'The team respect you. That's hard to win but easily lost. You're never really off duty.' She got hold of Janine's glass, edged it away.

'That's right,' Janine said, 'you can be all mates together, nice and chummy and next morning you're in the office giving someone a bollocking.' *Like someone not a million miles away.* Janine reached over for her drink and took a swig. She'd just finish this one, wouldn't do any harm.

'You have to set the tone, lead by example,' Louise Hogg said carefully, 'it can be tricky, knowing where to draw the line. And a case like this — it's hard for everyone involved.'

'You can say that again. We're all working our balls off and getting nowhere. I'm telling the parents of a missing three-year-old that I've still no news and it makes me wonder if maybe I'm doing something wrong. Maybe I can't hack it anymore. Am I just in the job because it's all I've ever done? And if I feel like this how am I going to keep up morale for that lot?'

Janine looked across to see the big lass in pink flouncing off, Butchers mopping at his face with a handkerchief. Didn't look like a match made in heaven. Her thoughts lit on Clive and Claire then Clive and Felicity, the way their marriage had soured and died, then on Pete. No, she admonished herself, I'm here for a good time and a good time is damn well what I'm going to have.

CHAPTER 17

Day Four: Thursday 1 May

Janine woke with a crushing headache, roiling guts and an uncomfortable sense of unease. She was too old, her liver too tired to cope with nights like that.

Charlotte was burbling in her cot. It was six am. Janine left her to burble and went to shower. Her mortification grew as snatches from the evening came back to haunt her, her ill-fated attempts to tease Richard and Millie that had quickly unravelled. And Louise! Oh, Lord. Louise warning Janine and Janine playing dumb. And then to crown it all she had confided in Louise, blurted out her doubts. 'Kids, promotion, a case like this. Usually, usually,' Janine had found it hard to pronounce the word right, 'I can hack it, wing and a prayer, yeah? Having it all, they call it having it all. Well . . . it's too bloody much, sometimes . . .'

'Do you need time off? It can be arranged.'

'Nah! Just having a moan, Louise, honestly, I can cope. I will cope. I want to get the bastard. Bastards. Plural.'

Shit! Had she offered to resign? Janine tested the notion but could not recall actually saying that.

Did she tell Louise about Pete and Tina and the baby? God, please, no. There were some parts of her life she'd rather keep private. Louise was OK but she didn't have kids, didn't have that extra load, day in and day out. Janine didn't know if that had been a conscious choice or whether it had just never happened or even whether it was something Louise had longed for that never came to pass. They weren't close enough for that sort of conversation.

Janine's toes curled and she felt heat on the nape of her neck as she imagined what she might have shared, blithely overstepping the boundaries under the influence.

There'd been some bother with Butchers too, not that she needed to feel any responsibility for Butchers' behaviour. She had enough on her own plate. Butchers and the fiancée had left the party early on and never returned. Maybe he'd gone after her to make up.

Janine wasn't sure she was right for him. Butchers had been married once before, had a child as well, but that had all gone wrong and he didn't see the child. It hadn't looked like there was much love lost last night. Kim seemed to treat him as a joke. Not a good way to start a marriage — no respect. Butchers could be an idiot but he wasn't a stupid man. Nor was he malicious. He played the clown at times, his size and demeanour made him an easy target for people's jokes but he was a diligent detective.

She thought of her own marriage. Did she still respect Pete? Not really. Certainly not the way he was dealing with the whole baby situation. She rinsed the shampoo from her hair wincing as the movement of her head backwards made the pounding behind her eyes even more violent.

She wouldn't have been so peevish with Millie if she and Richard hadn't been so condescending, as if suddenly instead of being Richard's old mate, pals and colleagues, Janine had turned into some embarrassing maiden aunt or alcoholic neighbour to be tolerated and evaded as quickly as possible, passed on to someone else to deal with.

As she turned off the shower, Charlotte cried for attention, a noise that pierced Janine's skull and made her grit her teeth. She needed coffee and painkillers. Janine put on a bathrobe and went to pick her daughter up and wondered how soon she could rouse the nanny.

* * *

She wasn't the only one suffering judging by the state of the rest of them. Apart from Detective Superintendent Hogg, of course, fresh as a daisy and looking critically at Janine as Janine got herself some water. Janine smiled hello, determined to keep up a front of normality even while her mind was scrabbling around wondering what else she might have said or done in her drunken stupor. Lesson one — do not get pissed in front of the boss.

Janine realized that she had left her laptop in the hall. Pete had stayed the night, bunking in the spare room, not something he did regularly but it meant he hadn't had to stay up late waiting for Janine to get home and as it was his day off today he could take Eleanor and Tom to school, which they always liked. She rang and got his voicemail and left a message asking him to drop her laptop off at the station once he'd done the school run.

Lisa and Butchers hadn't arrived as she began the briefing on the murder. Not like either of them. Butchers had never been late in all the years she'd worked with him, and Lisa keen and energetic, wouldn't dare be late, too eager to make the grade.

'News has come through from Interpol,' she told the team, 'Dutch police have completed the comparison on the DNA profiles of missing Tomas Rink and our unknown victim. No match.' Janine knew it had been a long shot, though she'd held out a sliver of hope because if the child had come in from another country, it would account for why no-one here had reported him missing.

'Those we know with easy access to the crime scene are the Palfreys, the Staffords and the builders McEvoy and Breeley. We now have detailed statements from them and we also have house-to-house for the whole of Kendal Avenue plus testimony from Royal Mail staff, window cleaners, meter readers, Avon lady, the works. That little lot needs correlating and mapping out.' The run of bad weather hadn't done them any favours. Fewer people had been out and about, and when they were they didn't linger. They were concerned with keeping dry, getting from A to B as quickly as possible. The heavy rain made it harder to see too, especially if you were driving. They'd got absolutely nowhere finding a primary crime scene. And without the identity of the child they had no idea where to look. 'Someone put that child there. They weren't observed, so when did they get the chance?'

'Paedos, boss.' Shap began.

'Sex offenders,' she corrected him.

'Them and all,' he grinned. 'Known individuals on the sex offenders register in the neighbourhood have been visited and interviewed. No-one's done a bunk or raised any alarm bells with their probation workers, apart from this one perv who admitted breaching his licence by being within a hundred yards of a school.'

'He admitted it?' Richard asked. 'Perhaps he owned up to that hoping to hide what he'd really been doing.'

Had this been the bearded weirdo by the gate?

'His story checked out,' Shap said. 'He'd travelled across town to Altrincham and spent the days indulging his fetid little fantasies outside a high school there. On the Saturday in question he did the same, loitering near the playing fields. His record's for raping twelve and thirteen-year-old girls.'

'A different profile from our victim,' Janine said. She was distracted by Lisa's arrival. 'Late night, Lisa?'

'I've been out with Sergeant Butchers, boss. He's brought in Luke Stafford and Phoebe Wray.'

What on earth! 'Has he now?' She felt a surge of irritation. She couldn't blame Lisa, Butchers was her senior in rank so if he said jump, Lisa or any other DC would have to, unquestioningly.

'Continue building a timeline for the crime scene and identify periods when the place was apparently deserted,' Janine told the team. 'There may have been opportunities for the killer to leave the body. Anyone need further guidance on tasks in hand see Sergeant Shap,' she wound up briskly. She set off to see just what the hell Butchers was playing at.

* * *

Butchers looked shocking, unshaven with a gash under his eye where presumably the fiancée had left her feedback.

'Why are they here?' Janine demanded, 'I expressly told you yesterday that you were to do nothing without some solid grounds.'

'They were at Luke Stafford's together on the Saturday afternoon,' Butchers said quickly. 'I've just asked her. That's where she went after the hockey match. Luke failed to mention it and her mother said she was at home, so she's lying as well. They could have gone to the park and taken Sammy back to Luke's. Stafford wouldn't let us search. If we can get a warrant—'

'You're clutching at straws,' Janine said, 'it's all supposition.'

'I know the lad's involved,' he insisted, 'they're alibi-ing each other.'

'You do not know,' Janine said. 'You *believe* he's involved. This is not a faith based operation, Butchers.'

'Don't you want to find out what they were doing together, why they kept that quiet,' he said.

'I can imagine,' Janine said crossly, 'I've a teenager at home. We can't talk to either of them without their parents present,' she said, 'and I'm not sure that's warranted—'

'The parents are here,' Butchers hurried to tell her. 'Well, Felicity Wray and Ken Stafford.'

Janine was tempted to tell him to send the lot of them away but relented. They should try and find out why the youngsters had been secretive, if only to rule them out of the picture and put a stop to Butchers' mission.

'If I can just interview them,' Butchers said.

'No way,' said Janine, 'you're convinced they're involved and that compromises your impartiality. I'll do it. Let's hope you're not wasting my time.'

CHAPTER 18

She began with Felicity and Phoebe. 'This is ridiculous,' Felicity Wray began as soon as Janine entered the interview room.

'Mrs Wray, Phoebe, I hope we won't keep you very long, just some anomalies I need to clear up.' The woman muttered and Janine reined in her own antipathy, Felicity Wray drove her barmy. How on earth her daughter put up with it, she had no idea.

Janine made introductions for the tape and stated the time then said, 'Phoebe, I want to talk to you about your movements on the day that Sammy went missing. After the hockey match—'

'I've already told you,' Felicity huffed and puffed.

'Mrs Wray, please, I'm asking Phoebe.' Janine turned back to the girl who was looking very wary. 'After the hockey match where did you go?'

'Luke's,' she said in a small voice. She looked terrified.

'Luke Stafford's?'

'Yes.'

Felicity Wray gave a theatrical gasp and shook her head, rattling her earrings. Janine saw the girl glance at her mother. Phoebe's mouth tightened, then she looked away.

'What did you do at Luke's?' Janine said.

'We hung out together, that's all. We just stayed at his house.'

'You didn't go out at all?'

'No,' Phoebe said.

'That boy's totally out of control,' Felicity said.

'You don't know anything about him,' Phoebe said.

'I know he's a violent thug!' Felicity retorted.

'That's rubbish,' Phoebe said, looking close to tears.

'Mrs Wray, please,' Janine intervened, 'let's hear what Phoebe has to say.'

'Luke's not a thug. His mum died and his dad won't even say her name. It's like she never existed. He's really down and people wind him up so he gets into fights, that's all.'

'That's all!' Felicity snorted with derision.

Janine glared at her. 'How far would he go?' Janine said to Phoebe. 'Has he ever really hurt anybody?'

'No, it's just a scrap — usually someone who's getting at him, they pick on him,' Phoebe said. 'He doesn't like fighting. And sometimes all he talks about is killing himself because his life's not worth living.'

'I know a great loss can—' Felicity began.

'Please!' Janine said, 'Be quiet.'

'No! No, it's not the same,' Phoebe confronted her mother. 'His mum died. Dad left you, right? Well, he left me too. You just made it harder. He wanted to see me but you made it impossible. You made me pick sides. You went on and on about it. Like it was only you that mattered, how he'd hurt you.' She stopped suddenly, eyes brimming, pressed her hand to her mouth.

Felicity looked stunned. She obviously wasn't used to Phoebe challenging her.

'Did anyone ever ask what you wanted after your parents separated?' Janine said.

Phoebe shook her head. 'I wasn't even allowed to talk to him. I missed him so much.'

'You should have told me,' Felicity said.

'Like you care,' Phoebe said.

'If I'd known—'

'Phoebe's telling you now,' Janine told Felicity, 'just listen.' She nodded to the girl who began to speak again, her eyes cast down, thumb picking at the table's edge. 'He'd gone and then you took the pills. What if I hadn't found you in time? Did you even think about that? And what it was like for me? I'm so sick of it. I just want it to stop.'

Janine saw Felicity's face alter, a tremor flickered around her mouth then her eyes filled. For an awful moment Janine thought she was going to break down, respond with histrionics to her daughter's plea for understanding but then Felicity Wray spoke quietly, 'I am sorry. It will stop. I promise.'

'I want to see Dad.'

Felicity opened her mouth, resistance in her face but then she sighed. 'OK, if you're sure but—'

'Mum!' Whatever Felicity's objection was Phoebe obviously didn't want to know.

'On the nineteenth of April,' Janine said, 'you and Luke, did you go to Withington park?'

'No,' Phoebe said.

'When was the last time you saw Sammy?'

'When Dad brought him round,' she said.

'And can you tell me anything at all about him going missing?' Janine said.

'No, honestly.' She sniffed.

Janine nodded. 'Has Luke spoken to you about the murder, the little boy found next door?'

'A bit — just how horrible it is.'

'Phoebe, we recovered a book from your room,' Janine lifted the envelope up and pulled out the book that Butchers had got so excited about.

Phoebe froze, an expression of horror in her eyes. 'It was for school,' she said quickly, 'for Crime and Punishment. It's on the reading list. That's all. I borrowed it from Luke.'

Janine slid the book away. 'Phoebe, why didn't you tell us before about going to Luke's?'

97

'Because of Mum, because she'd tell me off,' she said, looking thoroughly miserable. 'I'm sorry, I really am.'

'OK,' Janine said. She believed the girl and she was sorry that she'd been put through the trauma of a police interview but perhaps there was a silver lining if Phoebe got to see her father as she wanted to.

CHAPTER 19

Claire almost laughed as she realized why she was feeling so sick. Hysteria wild in her chest. This wasn't sorrow or the nausea of grief. She was pregnant. They had been trying for a few months, ready to add to the family, to have a brother or sister for Sammy. Now they no longer even had Sammy.

Claire felt like smashing something, hurling the vase on the windowsill, with its fancy bouquet of decorative dried grasses and seed pods, at the mirror and watching the cascade of silver glass. The resounding crash of broken dreams.

It felt like a vicious irony. An appallingly distasteful joke. How could she possibly nurture a baby, let it grow inside her, when her whole world was so empty?

She heard Clive in the kitchen downstairs. The family liaison officer wouldn't be here today, though they could always call if they needed her. The mornings were hard, waking to remember. Waking to the absence, not to hear Sammy giggling, or to have him clambering all over them. But the nights were worse. It was then that the vilest thoughts plagued her. At first she tried not to imagine what might be happening to him, to block it out but she simply couldn't sustain it. So she let the demons in, cobbled together scenarios snatched from bleak television documentaries or in-depth newspaper features she'd seen in the past. The trade in children. The court cases that sickened yet fascinated. Sometimes she prayed that he was dead rather than suffering.

'Claire,' Clive called up, 'do you want tea?'

She laughed to herself. What earthly use was tea?

She didn't reply but instead went downstairs to the drinks cabinet. Poured herself a half-tumbler full of vodka.

Clive came in and saw. 'Bit early, isn't it?'

'Does it matter?' she said. 'Does anything actually really matter anymore?'

Clive shrugged. His expression softened as he moved towards her but she held up her hand to stop him.

'I'm sorry,' Clive said. 'How many more times? I messed up but I was just trying to see my daughter. Is that so very wrong?'

'You should have stayed with them,' Claire said.

'I love you, I don't love Felicity,' he said.

'Then why do you come running like a fucking poodle every time she whistles?'

'I don't,' he said hotly.

'When I had Sammy—'

'Not that, not still that,' he groaned. 'It wasn't her I was going to. It was Phoebe. She was eleven years old. I am her father.'

Claire drank, the heat of the alcohol searing through her belly, spreading into the back of her skull.

'Don't shut me out,' he reached a hand towards her but she batted it away.

'I'm pregnant,' she said.

'What?' Shock slackened his face. 'But . . . well . . .' His eyes lit up, a half smile tugged at his lips. 'That's wonderful.'

How could he say that? Think that? 'No,' she said, 'it really isn't.'

His eyes moved to the glass in her hand. She drained it dry. Reached for the bottle, already feeling unsteady. When had she last eaten?

'I can't have it,' she said.

'Claire!'

'I can't. You want me to just substitute this baby for Sammy. No!'

'You're talking rubbish,' he said, 'that's not what I meant at all. We wanted another baby, we talked about it—'

'That was before,' she poured another drink. Her mouth watered, a sour taste mixed with the astringent sting of the alcohol.

'Please Claire,' he said, 'don't decide yet, not like this. It's a shock with everything else that's . . . I love you,' he said.

The silence that followed was deafening. Did she love him? She honestly couldn't tell any more, she was so angry with him, so confused.

'I don't want to lose you too,' he said quietly.

'You should have thought about that when you lied to me, lied to the—'

'All right!' he exploded. 'I know. I fucked up. I made mistakes. Don't you think I regret that every second of the day?' He was shouting, he flung his arms wide, turned in a half circle and back. 'I don't want to be that man. The man who messes up. My first marriage was a disaster and I should have come down harder on Felicity, I know that now. I should have fought for custody but I thought we could come to some arrangement. Maybe I can't change but I want you and I want Sammy back and I want this new baby. I am sick of feeling like this, feeling like I've let you down. But I will not spend the rest of my life being punished for it. Just like you should stop punishing yourself. You didn't take Sammy. You're not to blame.'

Claire felt as though he had kicked her.

'Whoever did take him, whoever that person is, don't let them take what we have left,' he said, his eyes locked on her. 'You don't want this baby because you don't feel you deserve it.'

Was that true? Claire gritted her teeth, determined not to break down. 'And if I get rid of it?'

'Honestly?' he said. 'I don't know.'

Hot tears burned behind her eyes.

'But I'm not going to play games anymore. Not with Felicity, not with you.' He turned away. 'I need some air.' And he left.

She cried again, feeling utterly bewildered and alone. Then she lifted the glass to take another swig and felt a spasm in her guts and a rush of vomit up her throat and the back of her nose. She reached the kitchen sink just in time and clung there until she was empty and spent.

* * *

Claire was sitting in the lounge when Clive came back in.

He took off his jacket and looked directly across at her.

'Do you think he's still alive?' she said.

'I don't know what I think,' said Clive, 'I have to believe he is. I have to hope.'

'Because then it might come true?' she said.

'Something like that.'

'If they come again, say they've found the body?' her voice shook.

'I hope they won't, that's all there is.'

She looked out of the window where it had begun to rain, thin drops scattered across the glass by the wind.

'Tea?' he said

She tried to smile, almost succeeded. 'Thanks. That'd be nice.' And she closed her eyes and listened to the pattering of the rain.

CHAPTER 20

Ken Stafford was fuming, Janine didn't blame him but she had to present a united front. 'Why on earth are we here?' the man said bitterly, a half snarl on his face, 'this is a bloody outrage.'

'There's a very good reason we're here,' Janine said calmly, 'we are conducting two very serious investigations. A child murder inquiry and a search for a missing child and when my officers spoke to you, Luke,' she looked the boy in the eyes and he glanced away, 'you failed to mention your connection to Phoebe Wray and you also failed to mention the fact that you and Phoebe spent time together on the day you were being asked about. Why was that?'

'They just asked me where I was,' Luke said defensively.

'Didn't you realise it might be significant, or that withholding such information might impede our inquiries and waste time?'

Luke shrugged, a blush crept up his neck, glowed in his cheeks.

'Luke, think carefully before you answer me now, do you know anything about the abduction of Sammy Wray?'

'No,' he said.

'Did you and Phoebe leave your house together that afternoon?'

'No.'

'What time did Phoebe arrive?' Janine said.

'About half-one.'

'And what time did she leave?'

'Four.'

'You didn't see Phoebe?' Janine checked with Mr Stafford.

'No, I was asleep, I work nights,' he said as though tired of repeating it.

'Did Phoebe say anything to you that day about Sammy?' she said to Luke.

'No . . . oh,' he caught himself, 'yes, she said she wished it wasn't all such a mess, that people could just get on. That maybe it would be cool having a little brother.' Janine thought of Tom and his fears about Pete and Tina's baby.

'And why did you not tell us about Phoebe being with you?'

'It's her mum,' he said, 'she's got it in for me.'

'She doesn't approve of your friendship?'

'No, she thinks Phoebe's too good for me,' he said.

'Is it more than a friendship, Luke?'

'What's that got to do with anything?' Ken Stafford broke in.

Janine ignored him. 'Luke?'

'We're just mates,' he said.

'An item was recovered from Phoebe Wray's possession.' Janine showed him the book. 'Is this yours?'

He swallowed. Paused. Don't deny it, thought Janine, it's got your name in, for God's sake.

'Yeah. It's just a book,' he said quickly.

'You were interested in it?'

'Yes. That's not a crime is it?' A flash of anger there and Janine wondered for a second exactly what Luke was capable of.

'No, but given the investigation I am interested in what made you buy a book like this.'

'We were doing crime and punishment — at school, in sociology. Stuff about the age of responsibility and that,' he said.

'And why give it to Phoebe?'

'Same — she's doing it as well.'

'What about the child found at the house next door, can you tell me anything about him?'

'No.' Alarm flared in his eyes. 'I swear. How can you think that?' He blinked hard and Janine saw how upset he was.

'Would you have any objection to giving us a hair and DNA sample to help eliminate you from the inquiry?' she said, thinking of the hair found in the sheet, short and dark like Luke's.

'You don't seriously think he had anything to do with it.' Ken Stafford got to his feet. 'That's absolutely ridiculous.'

'Please, sit down,' Janine said.

'I can't believe you people—'

'Mr Stafford, please sit down. This isn't helping.'

He sat and Janine said, 'Would you be prepared to give us a hair and DNA sample, Luke?'

Luke looked to his father. Ken Stafford rolled his eyes and flung up his hands. 'What does that involve?'

'We take a mouth swab from Luke and a couple of hairs from his head. It will only take a few minutes.'

Luke nodded.

'Is there anything else you wish to say?' Janine asked him.

'No.'

She paused a moment, in case he volunteered any more, but although his face was working, and he chewed on the inside of his lip he didn't speak again. 'Is there any detail you remember that you didn't tell us in your earlier statement, anything about comings and goings at the house next door, any unusual activity, noises late at night, people you didn't recognise in the area, anything at all?'

'No. Where's Phoebe?' Luke said.

'She's going home with her mum,' Janine said.

'She's all right?' Luke said, his voice almost breaking with relief. Janine felt like hugging him, the poor, daft lad.

'Yes,' Janine said, 'thanks for your help. Can you just wait outside for a minute, in the other room?'

Once Luke had left, Janine said, 'The problems that Luke's been having — they started after your wife's death?'

'What problems?' Ken Stafford said with hostility.

'Fighting, suspension from school and so on.'

Ken Stafford looked uncomfortable, 'He took it hard.'

'Did you try and talk to him? Did he get any help?'

Ken Stafford shuffled in his chair. 'There's no point in dwelling on it.'

'So you did nothing,' said Janine. 'Are you aware that Luke's struggling with depression?'

'Kids that age—'

'Mr Stafford this isn't some teenage tantrum. Luke has been having suicidal thoughts.'

'Who told you that,' he said as though he didn't believe it.

'That doesn't matter. What does matter, what is important is that Luke gets some support before it's too late. He seems like a decent enough lad, he could make something of himself but that's unlikely if he's left to flounder.'

'He wouldn't—' he said but the belligerence had evaporated. It was sinking in.

'It happens,' Janine said, 'far too often. And sometimes for what seem to be the most trivial reasons. Losing a parent, that's not trivial. Have you heard of CAMHS?' she pronounced it *calms*. 'Child and Adolescent Mental Health Service.'

He shook his head.

'I'll give you their details,' Janine said, 'they are very good.'

'Thank you,' he said quietly. He'd gone pale. Janine thought he probably needed some therapy himself. He'd clearly not got over the bereavement either. Still, one step at a time.

'Oh, God,' he shuddered, his thoughts obviously still on the awful prospect of suicide.

'We'll get those samples taken now,' Janine said, 'won't take long and you can get home.'

He nodded, got to his feet slowly, his earlier antagonism replaced by bewilderment.

CHAPTER 21

DCI Lewis was spitting mad. Butchers stood in her office and took it.

'I'm a detective chief inspector not a bloody family therapist. You drag them in here, forcing me to take time away from two critical investigations. Neither of them have anything to do with it, except in your fevered imagination. You latched onto Luke Stafford, the whole teenage killers theory, and made it your mission because it was easier than dealing with personal stuff.' She shook her head irritably. 'We've all done it but it cocks things up. Here, and at home.'

'Sorry boss,' he said. 'It's all off — the engagement.'

'Now, why am I not surprised? Happy?'

Butchers shrugged. Relief if he had to put a name to it, blessed relief. 'She was a bit of a slapper,' he said.

'And you're a prat. Now, you did door-to-door at the Staffords, I want to review your original statements, see how objective they are. Get them now,' she barked. 'And don't pull any stunts like this again. I decide who we pull in and when. Got it?'

'Yes boss.'

He was out of there.

* * *

Pete arrived with her laptop in time to hear the tail end of Janine setting Butchers straight. Janine was still angry. With Butchers. With Pete. And her headache had grown worse not better.

'Laying down the law?' Pete said. 'Looks like he's done a few rounds with Amir Khan.'

He held up the laptop and she took it and put it on the desk, plugged it in.

'Thank you would be nice,' Pete said.

Any show of restraint that she had intended went out of the window. 'Honesty would be nice,' she snapped. 'Were you ever going to say anything? Telling the kids and getting them to do it — how pathetic is that!'

'I didn't tell them,' Pete said affronted, 'it was Tina.' *It wasn't me! Like a five-year-old.*

'Oh, so you were keeping the baby secret from all of us? Forgive me if I don't congratulate you.' She wanted to punch him, to slap him.

'I don't want another child,' Pete said making eye contact, 'you know that. It was never part of the plan. Look,' he said more softly, 'whatever happens I'm not going anywhere. The kids — I'll be here for them.'

'How are you going to fit it all in?' she said.

'I'll have to find a way,' he blustered.

'So, is she going to want to get married?' Janine said.

'I don't know,' Pete said, as though he was fed up with the whole situation.

'Oh, go on, Pete, take a wild guess. What is it? A commitment too far?'

'It's not just the baby,' Pete said, 'it's just — I had options. See how things panned out.'

Talk about pathetic.

'And you can't leave Tina now, can you?' Janine said. 'But no, hang on! You left me when I was carrying Charlotte. Don't tell me you've suddenly developed principles. Options!' She could feel the rage burning behind her breastbone, her temperature rising. 'And what options did I have? Promotion, three kids and one on the way when you swan off. I didn't choose this. It wasn't in my plan.' It came to her then, what she did want. She wanted rid of Pete, she wanted to seal the separation. He wasn't ever coming back, things were never going to be how they used to be.

'I want a divorce,' Janine said.

Pete was taken aback. 'You're upset,' he said.

'You don't say! But I've had enough Pete. It's been two years, it's not complicated. This isn't a marriage. It's over.' She knew how final it was. Felt a moment's sadness that this was how it ended, with an ill-tempered squabble in her place of work, prompted by his cowardice and fuelled by him whining about his lot.

'Janine—' he said, moving closer as though to reason with her but she cut him dead, 'I'll set things in motion.' She opened the laptop and sat down to work, 'And I'll tell the kids,' she couldn't resist adding as he moved to go.

* * *

Janine read carefully through the statements. It wasn't as bad as she feared, apparently Butchers' years of experience in taking down factual information had served him well. The initial statements were quite bald, perhaps because, as Butchers had said and Janine could imagine, the Staffords were surprisingly uncooperative. Now she knew it wasn't so much that they had an agenda, a reason to mislead the police but more that father and son were too bound up in their own misery to engage. Of course those initial statements were made at a time when everyone was imagining that the dead child was Sammy Wray.

It was hard now to pull apart the two cases, as if the details resisted being untangled. It made any analysis more complicated.

Janine froze, the skin on the back of her neck prickled and she took a quick breath. *Woken by the builders.* Wasn't that a contradiction? She rifled through the statements. Yes. There. She found the other reference.

She picked up the pages and went to the door of her office. Called out to the team. 'Statements from Ken Stafford — second statement, quote: "Saturday, back from the night shift, just got off to sleep when the builders start up." Luke Stafford tells us his dad complained about it.' She pulled out the other page. 'The initial door-to-door testimony from Ken Stafford, and I quote, "Don't see them for days, then they'd turn up at the crack of dawn". Join the dots. If they are so bloody lazy then why do they suddenly pitch up at the crack of dawn on a Saturday morning? Lazy builders on the job before daylight. It's the builders we should be talking to. The bloody builders!'

CHAPTER 22

'Breeley and McEvoy,' Janine said, 'pull together everything we have so far, every whisper, every mention we have of them and do background checks. I'll give you half an hour then we'll see what it tells us.'

When they re-assembled Janine got the ball rolling. 'Both men have been working on the site for six weeks. Owner's abroad?'

'That's right,' said Lisa, 'we spoke to him to verify that. And he's hired them before and had no complaints.'

'OK, starting with Joe Breeley,' Janine said. 'Breeley has an alibi for the early hours of Saturday morning from his wife. If it is him — his wife is covering. Breeley has an alibi, but Donny McEvoy doesn't. McEvoy lives alone, no family.'

'That make it any more likely?' Richard said.

'No-one keeping tabs on him,' Janine said.

'Has its advantages,' Richard muttered. Although he was contributing, he kept giving her dirty looks and his manner was decidedly frosty. To do with last night, she assumed.

'Breeley was fixing the car when we first went round,' Richard said, 'their car broke down, on the Friday afternoon, the eighteenth of April. AA were called out. Mandy was driving. So if that was out of action, if it was Breeley, he'd have used his van to move the body to the site.'

'From?' said Janine. Shrugs and shakes of the head. If only they knew. She thought about her visit to the Breeleys, had there been anything off-key?

'Breeley had been on the sick,' she said.

'Yes,' Richard agreed, 'that's what he said at first then he changed his story, said that the weather was slowing work down at the house so he hadn't been in.'

'Bit odd,' Janine said, 'young family to feed, and he's a steady reputation, wouldn't you want to be bringing in the money?'

'Might be paid for the job. Do the hours as and when,' said Butchers. 'Common enough in the building trade.'

'Yes, he said as much,' she remembered. 'Anything else on Breeley?'

No-one spoke. 'OK then, Donny McEvoy.'

Shap said, 'McEvoy was already at Kendal Avenue when Breeley turned up for work on that Saturday. Plus McEvoy was there when the body was recovered, he didn't actually find the body but . . .'

'He's shown a very public interest in the case,' Janine said. That type of close involvement was a feature of killers on occasion, a combination of fascination they had with the awful deed they'd committed, a need to be at the centre of attention but also a useful way they could keep tabs on what the police were doing. 'Is he just after his fifteen minutes or is there more to it? He's been eager to talk to us so far . . .'

She looked at Shap who nodded.

'Right see if he's happy for us to take a look round his place.'

'The murder scene?' Lisa asked.

'Worth a look,' Janine said, 'anything to suggest the victim was there. Or at the other site where McEvoy's been working? Find out if he's access there out of hours. We ask both men in turn about that early morning visit on Saturday nineteenth. Given the fact that McEvoy has no alibi and he's been rubber-necking I think we have grounds to bring him in and talk to him here. Shake him up a bit. Let's get cracking.'

As the meeting broke up she was aware of the tension between herself and Richard. She could have ignored it but she didn't want it to fester. 'Richard?' she said, 'A word?'

She moved with him to her office, made sure to shut the door, hoping for privacy.

'Is this about last night?' Janine said.

'What?' he said.

'This: the glacial tone, the moody stare? Did I pop your balloon?'

He rolled his eyes. 'You were a right cow to Millie. You could barely say her name, 'Millie,' he mimicked Janine. 'Patronising her, sticking your nose in. Maybe you don't remember? That was just before you made a complete prat of yourself with the boss. What is your problem with Millie? Is she some sort of threat?' Richard was livid, hands on hips, his eyes burning.

'I work with her, I don't have to like her,' Janine said. 'Have you seen today's papers?' They were making much of the confusion of the cases, pointing the finger at the police.

'You're blaming Millie for the coverage?' he said, incredulously. 'She's doing her best in a very difficult situation. You know what that's like, to be up against it. You've been there.'

He was right. She had been there, got the DVD. She was being a cow because she was pissed off with Pete. Pete and bloody Tina. And Millie, with her poise and her brains, her youthful beauty and her claim on Richard, had been a handy target. She missed her mate Richard, she missed the buzz there used to be between them, the easy company, the patter and the unspoken support. She winced as she recalled bawling out Richard over talking to Millie about the case and then omitting to inform Millie about Felicity Wray's arrest. Petty behaviour. She wasn't being straight with him. Janine swallowed. She did not want to be like this, act like this. As if she was no longer in control.

'It's just,' she said, 'I'm just—' she looked away, down the corridor.

'What?' he said irritably.

'Tina's having a baby,' she blurted it out. 'Pete always told me he didn't want any more children. That was something we had. He didn't even have the bottle to tell me himself,' she said sadly, 'I had to hear it from the kids. I hate the whole idea of it.'

'But you and Pete, it's finished, right?' he said, some confusion in his eyes.

She sighed. 'I've told him I want a divorce.'

He was still puzzled. He didn't get it, he really didn't get it. 'Well, what d'you expect,' he said, 'you can't have it both ways.'

Janine was stung. Before she'd formulated a response Richard had walked out. Well, that went well, she told herself. She felt like crying but contented herself with kicking her desk, which brought tears to her eyes.

She was startled by a knock on the door. Christ! Couldn't she have five minutes peace? She sniffed hard, sat down. 'Yes?' she said.

Millie opened the door. 'I'd a voicemail from Richard, I thought he was here. Sorry to bother you,' she said formally, making to leave again.

'Come in,' Janine said. 'We've had a break, he probably wanted to tell you — Ken Stafford's statement puts one of the builders at the scene early Saturday morning.'

'Who?' Millie said, alert.

'Can't eliminate either of them yet,' Janine said.

'Anything else?' Millie said.

Was she expecting an apology? Janine felt discomfited but decided that keeping it all professional was the best way forwards. 'You could issue a statement: new information has given us some positive leads. I'm very hopeful.'

'That true?' Millie said.

Was it? Hardly. Janine didn't dare to be very hopeful any more. Hope was a scarce commodity. 'No. It feels like

I'm smacking my head against a brick wall, actually, but that doesn't scan so well.'

'I could dig around a bit, do an archive search?'

Janine accepted the offer. It felt like an olive branch of sorts. 'Thanks, that'd be great.'

Janine watched her go. She was so pretty, young too, Janine guessed a good ten years younger than Richard and her. And obviously good at her job. *And am I not*, Janine asked herself. Where had all her confidence gone? All that energy and conviction?

CHAPTER 23

McEvoy sat beside a duty solicitor and Janine was sure he was still enjoying the attention. He made a show of watching keenly as she loaded the tape and did the preamble to the interview.

'I'd like to talk to you about your whereabouts on the nineteenth of April, the Saturday,' Janine said. 'In your statement you said you arrived for work at approximately nine am.'

'That's right,' McEvoy said.

'We have a witness who heard work start at Kendal Avenue much earlier,' Janine told him and watched his face change, the expression of avid interest changing to one of consternation.

'It can't have been me. I didn't get there till nine,' McEvoy insisted.

'Were you the first?' Janine said.

'Yes,' said McEvoy

'When did Joe Breeley show?' Richard asked.

'Just after. You think he might have something to do with it?' McEvoy leant forward, mouth forming a salacious smile.

'You're the one in the interview room,' Richard pointed out.

'That's bollocks,' McEvoy reared back. 'I went round to sort out the flood on Monday, I was the one reported it. Why would I do that?' He looked askance.

'You tell me,' Richard said.

McEvoy said nothing and for the first time Janine felt he was taking on board the seriousness of the situation.

'You're a true crime fan, am I right?' Richard said.

McEvoy nodded.

'You'll know then, that there are some people who attract particular attention in a murder inquiry,' Richard continued.

McEvoy couldn't resist showing off. He nodded eagerly, 'Family and close friends.'

'Also the last person to see the victim alive, the one who finds the body, anybody showing an excessive interest in the case and a person who returns to the scene of the crime,' Richard said.

'That's three out of four,' Janine said unsmiling.

'No way,' McEvoy shouted. 'You've got it arse over tits. I was working there and I called in the flood. That's just circumstantial that is.'

'You've been trying to sell your story to the papers. What exactly is your story?' Janine said.

'It's human interest, it's in the public domain,' he said. Then he became defensive. 'I'm entitled—'

'What vehicle do you use for work?' Richard said.

'An old transit,' McEvoy said.

'Diesel?'

'Yeah, why?'

'Handy that — if you wanted to move something, hide something,' Richard said

'I'm not hiding anything,' McEvoy said hotly.

'As you know we have a team searching your house. Are we going to find anything there?' Richard said.

'No, nothing, nothing at all.' He wasn't smiling anymore.

'Do you know who the child is?' Janine asked.

'No! Look, you've got it all wrong,' he said, 'the papers, and that, I was just trying to help. That's all.'

He stuck unwaveringly to his account of arriving at work on that day at nine and no earlier. As the interview went on he pleaded with them to believe him. 'Honest, on my mother's grave,' he said more than once.

They let him go with a warning that they might well want to speak to him again.

'What do you think?' she said to Richard.

He shrugged, shook his head. 'Don't know.'

No, she thought, *neither do I.*

* * *

The Breeleys were both home when Janine and Richard called on them.

'Hello Joe, Mandy. Can we come in?' Janine said.

A friendly smile from Joe Breeley but Janine saw his throat ripple as he swallowed. Who really wants the police in the house — unless you're a victim needing assistance?

'We wanted to talk to you again about Saturday the nineteenth of April. You got to Kendal Avenue just after nine, how long after?'

'Maybe quarter past,' he said.

'And Donny McEvoy was already there?' said Janine.

'That's right,' he said.

'And how did Mr McEvoy seem?'

'Same as usual,' Joe Breeley said, 'why?' He looked concerned.

'You were here at home till then?' Janine asked.

'Yes,' he said.

'You can confirm that?' she turned to Mandy.

'Yes, he was.' She tried to smile but it was a weak attempt.

'Are you certain about that?' Janine said.

'Yes,' Mandy replied, 'it was me had to tell him to get up, he went back to sleep after the alarm.'

'And you didn't go to work on the Monday,' Richard said, 'why was that?'

'The rain—' he began but Mandy cut him off.

'It's OK, Joe, we just tell them the truth.'

Janine felt a tightening in her chest. Joe Breeley had been hiding something.

'It was me,' Mandy said, 'I was struggling with the kids, not coping and then the car had broken down and . . .' Her mouth trembled as she spoke. 'I asked him to stay off, help me,' she sounded close to tears.

Janine could remember those early days, broken nights, the never-ending demands of small children, how hard it was to keep on top of even the basics — feeding, changing, cleaning, shopping. The exhaustion.

'I didn't want to tell Donny,' Joe Breeley looked embarrassed, 'said my back had gone.'

Janine could well imagine the ribbing the single man would have given Breeley had he known the facts: she got you under her thumb? Not letting you out?

'Sorry,' Breeley added.

'OK,' Janine said. She glanced at the clock it was time to go, get herself to Withington Park for the reconstruction.

'The manhole cover over the sewer, how easy would it be for someone to remove it?' she said.

'Easy enough, just jemmy it up,' Joe Breeley said.

'Had you or Mr McEvoy any reason to open the cover in the course of the work you were doing?'

'No, that'd be a plumber's job. We're making good the fabric of the place, roof, walls, getting ready for the windows.'

Janine stood up. 'If anything else occurs to you, please let us know. Doesn't matter how small, how insignificant it might seem.'

'Donny,' Joe Breeley said, frowning, 'you don't think, you can't—'

'Routine inquiries,' Richard said,' we have to pin all the detail down. That's all.'

'Right,' Breeley said, 'course.' He smiled again but worry lingered in his eyes.

CHAPTER 24

The day was grey and blustery as the actors took their places getting ready to re-enact Sammy's abduction. A throng of press and media waited at a designated spot on the edge of the playground. A police officer was playing the part of Claire and Millie had found the son of a friend of a friend to play Sammy. They were dressed like Claire and Sammy had been on that sunny Saturday, right down to Sammy's glasses and distinctive red shoes. Janine shivered, the boy would be cold once they took his fleece off, but only for a few minutes. She stood with Claire and Clive and Millie. The couple huddled close together, Clive had his arm around Claire and she was clutching Sammy's fleece.

'We've a good turn out,' Janine said to Claire. The woman's face was wretched, hollowed and grey. There was a glassy, remote look in her eyes. Had she given up? Given up daring to hope?

The guilt must be crippling, thought Janine. To know that Sammy had disappeared while she was supposed to be looking after him. Janine wondered if the abduction had been premeditated or opportunistic. Had someone been watching Claire and Sammy, set their sights on the young boy, trailed them to the shops, to playgroup, to the park. Noting their routines and behaviour. Planned when to strike, a vehicle at the ready for a quick getaway, somewhere lined up to take the child, the whole thing done with intent and deliberation.

Or had there been a terrible collision of circumstances. A predator passing through the park, keen not to attract interest, window shopping if you like, just turned out to be in the right place at the right time, within feet of Sammy as his mother was distracted. A matter of seconds to pick up the child and walk steadily away.

Millie spoke to one of her colleagues who was co-ordinating the re-enactment. The actor playing Claire took the fleece from the child and led him round to the steps.

'He took his fleece off,' Claire said. 'Sammy always gets hot running about. But it was warm, it was really warm. He's only got his t-shirt now. What if he's cold?' Anxiety danced in her eyes. 'I should have gone to the front as soon as he got to the top of the slide.'

'Claire, I can't tell you what you want to hear,' Janine said. 'I'm so sorry. I wish I could. That's why today matters. If we can jog someone's memory—'

'What if it doesn't work?' Clive Wray said. 'How much longer—' he broke off, unable to continue.

Janine couldn't answer that question, either. Some children were never found. That was the reality. 'We're doing everything we can,' she said, 'I promise.'

The little boy pulled at the spectacles, unused to them. The woman playing Claire, took his hand and led him round again. The cameras drank it up, ready for broadcast on the news bulletins, for Crimewatch, for stills in the next editions of the papers, for the police website.

Janine looked at the T-shirt, the green dinosaur, just the sort of thing she'd have bought Tom when he was younger and obsessed with the creatures. She thought of the victim, the paltry evidence they had from the scene, everything compromised by the water and the actions of scavenging animals. The t-shirt, underpants, bed sheet, the human hairs and the screw. A glasses screw.

The boy slid down the slide and was caught at the bottom.

Janine's pulse jumped. She turned to Millie, and stepped closer, away from the Wrays so they wouldn't hear. 'The glasses screw in the sheet — we thought it was Sammy's,' Janine said, 'switch it round. What if that's the killer's?'

Millie understood straight away and nodded quickly.

Janine pulled out her phone and called Richard. 'Richard, the glasses screw, not that many three-year-olds wear glasses. It's more likely to be the killer's, isn't it? Get someone onto McEvoy, check the prescription of his glasses against the glass on the drive. He had his glasses on earlier but maybe he has a spare pair.'

'Or got them fixed,' Richard said.

'What about Joe Breeley, he wasn't wearing glasses, was he?'

'No,' said Richard. 'But if he'd broken them . . .'

'OK. Keep in touch, I shouldn't be much longer here and then we'll decide what we do next.'

* * *

'No match to McEvoy's prescription,' Richard told her as she arrived back at the office. 'And nothing out of order at his house.'

'Back to Breeley then,' she said.

'How do you want to play it?'

'Cautiously,' Janine didn't want to make any more mistakes.

Janine looked at the photographs, Joe and Mandy and their two sons. John and Aidan as newborns and older. In several photographs Joe Breeley was wearing glasses, rectangular, dark frames. Janine looked at Richard, signalled with her eyes. He saw what she meant, gave a brief nod.

Mandy was holding Aidan, she looked nervous, full of fleeting smiles.

123

'You've not got your glasses, Mr Breeley?' Richard said.

'I lost them,' Breeley said, 'I can manage without, don't need them really.'

'When was that, then, that you lost them?' said Richard.

'I can't remember.' He scratched at the edge of his jaw line.

'You didn't have them when we first called round. So, before then?' Richard said.

'He only needs them for reading. He's always losing them,' Mandy said. Aidan wriggled in her arms and squealed and she hushed him.

If he only needed the glasses for reading, Janine thought, then why was he wearing them in the photographs?

Breeley's leg was dancing, the man was wound up tight.

'We found optical glass on the pavement at Kendal Avenue. And a glasses screw inside the sheet the child was wrapped in. Your glasses — are they lost, or broken?' said Janine.

'Lost. I told you.'

'Maybe they're in the van,' said Richard, 'it's just out there. We can have a look.'

'No.' He got to his feet quickly. 'They're not there.'

'Won't take a minute,' Richard said, 'and we can clear this up.' Richard set off with Joe rushing after him, Janine and Mandy close behind.

'No!' Breeley was shouting, 'You don't go near my van.' Breeley tried to grab Richard, pull him back but Richard, the bigger man shrugged him off.

'No. Leave it!'

Richard reached the van and glanced in, turned back. 'Here all along, one lens broken.'

'It's nothing!' Breeley shouted, 'Just a pair of specs.'

Richard pulled handcuffs out and moved quickly to Breeley. Began the caution, 'Joseph Breeley, I am arresting you on suspicion of murder. You do not have to say anything . . .'

Mandy, her mouth open, was shaking her head. Then she began to shout, 'Leave him alone, get off him, he hasn't done anything. Leave him.' The baby was crying and Janine steered them back towards the house. 'Leave him alone,' Mandy shouted, 'where are you taking him?'

'He'll be at City Central Police Station while he helps us with our inquiries,' Janine said. 'We may wish to speak to you in due course.'

'I can't,' Mandy said, 'the kids . . . what about the kids?'

'If necessary we can provide temporary child care while we speak to you if you can't find anyone yourself.'

'He didn't . . . he couldn't . . .' she broke down.

Denying everything. Had she suspected her husband of such a crime? She had given him the alibi for the Saturday morning. Maybe that was genuine. The child could have been placed there another day, though that didn't account for the noise of the van heard so early in the day.

Or maybe Mandy Breeley suspected her husband but wouldn't admit it to herself. Shut down the whispers in her head, made light of the worry gnawing away inside. Wanted to believe him innocent. To believe he was a good man, a decent man. Not think that the father of her children murdered another child.

CHAPTER 25

While Joe Breeley was booked in and a solicitor was arranged, Janine and Richard prepared the interview, going over all the facts, the evidence they had and the contradictions in what Breeley had told them so far.

Janine had sent CSIs to recover the van. In the lab, Joe Breeley's glasses prescription was being compared to the broken lens found close to the manhole, and an examination was underway to see if the glasses screw fit the frames. In the custody suite, Breeley was being processed, having his fingerprints taken, giving a DNA sample and a hair from his head. The lab would look at the hair to see if it resembled the one recovered from inside the sheet. A DNA profile would establish if they came from the same person.

Once word came back positive on the screw and the lens prescription, Janine felt a wash of relief and the kick of excitement. Finally, finally they were getting closer, things were adding up. Still a lot of blanks to fill in but if they could just get Joe Breeley talking.

His solicitor was a whey faced woman with greasy hair. Thankfully she had not advised her client to offer no comment, perhaps because of the seriousness of the crime. She sat next to Breeley and opposite Richard and Janine in the interview room.

'What can you tell me about the body of a child recovered from Kendal Avenue on the twenty-eighth of April?' Janine said to Breeley.

'Nothing. I don't know anything about it, I swear,' he said.

'How do you account for the fact that a screw of the same type to that missing from your glasses was found in the sheet wrapped around the child's body?'

'I don't know.'

'You told us before that the manhole cover had been closed and that you had no need to access the drainage tunnel. So how come your glasses screw ends up in the drain, inside the sheet covering the child.'

'I don't know,' he said, looking away.

Janine could see a pulse ticking fast at the side of his neck.

'We have a witness who heard your vehicle arriving at the address at six-fifteen on the morning of the nineteenth of April,' Richard said.

The solicitor interrupted, 'Is this witness able to distinguish individual vehicles by the sound of their engines?'

Janine knew it was a fair point.

'A diesel engine, a sound the neighbours had become familiar with over the course of the weeks you were working there,' Richard said.

'I was at home then,' Breeley said.

'I don't think that's the case. When did you break your glasses?' Richard said.

'I don't remember.'

'Where did it happen?' Richard said.

'Not at work,' he replied.

'The screw must have worked loose, dropped onto the sheet. Later, as you were moving the body, your lens fell out and broke,' said Richard.

'It's not mine,' Joe Breeley said. He rubbed his jaw.

'We can identify the prescription from the fragments. It matches yours,' Richard said.

'You're bound to find traces of me all over the shop. I worked there,' Joe Breeley said.

'But you have just told us that you didn't break your glasses at work. I'm confused,' Janine said.

'You went to work early, in the van,' Richard said, 'you put the little boy there, left. Came back at nine. What happened, Joe?'

He refused to answer.

'How did particles of glass that match your missing lens come to be on the driveway at Kendal Avenue?' Richard said.

He shook his head. 'I don't know.' Temper or desperation edged his reply.

'We've taken a DNA sample from you along with hair from your head. Will we find that matches material recovered from the victim?'

Breeley stilled though Janine was not sure why but then he recovered. Had he remembered something incriminating? She decided to push this topic a bit further.

'Anything like that could have come from the house,' he said, 'we use the basin, the toilet.'

'And how might that have got inside the sheet? Or onto the child's body?' she said.

He swallowed, closed his eyes momentarily. 'I don't know.'

'Let's back up a little. Friday afternoon, the eighteenth of April. You left early?' Janine said.

'Yeah, Mandy was going shopping. I had the kids.'

'She didn't take them?' Janine said.

'No — John's got the chickenpox,' he said.

'So Mandy went shopping, she came back when?'

'She was late — the car broke down. Be going on five when she got back.'

'And that evening where were you?' Janine said.

'Just in the house,' Breeley said.

'Neither of you went out?' Janine said.

'No, honestly. Ask Mandy. She'll tell you,' he said.

'Oh, we will,' Janine said, 'I promise you that. Saturday morning what time did you leave home?'

'Nine o'clock, like I said.'

Joe Breeley maintained his story, refusing to be drawn, then there was a knock at the door. Richard suspended the interview, paused the tape and went to answer it.

He came back into the room and nodded to Janine. It must be something important.

'We'll take a break now, half an hour,' she said to the solicitor.

'You're keeping me here?' Joe Breeley said.

'For as long as it takes,' Janine replied.

'Millie's found something in Breeley's background,' Richard said in the corridor once Breeley had been escorted to a cell.

'Where is she?'

'Incident room.'

Millie held a sheaf of printouts. She handed Janine the top one. Janine scanned the headline. *Tot's Death Inquest.* She checked the date, 12th February 1991. Janine started to read, *The county coroner opened an inquest yesterday into the death of Gary Breeley (3) who died at the family home in October 1990.*

'Fractured skull,' said Millie. 'Joe Breeley had a little brother, Gary. Joe was looking after him when Gary died. He fell down some steps, fractured his skull. They ruled accidental death, though there were rumours.'

'Did he fall, or was he pushed?' said Janine.

'Exactly,' said Millie, 'Joe was ten at the time.'

The same cause of death. What were the chances? Was family man Breeley repeating an earlier crime?

'We can use this,' she said to Richard, 'we should put this to him.'

While they waited for the half hour to elapse, Janine checked on responses to the Sammy Wray reconstruction. 'The phones are red hot,' Shap told her, which could mean anything or nothing. Perhaps Sammy had been snatched and taken abroad, at best for an illegal adoption and at worst as a victim for the men who get pleasure from abusing children.

'Joe,' Janine said once they had resumed the interview, 'we really need to sort this out. You need to start telling us the truth. We have good reason to believe that you were involved in the death of the child found at Kendal Avenue. You've not been in to work since. Bad back you said, then excuses about the weather, then you claimed you stayed at home to help Mandy. Not like you to blob work according to Donny McEvoy. This is why, isn't it, Joe? You couldn't do it. Go back and carry on knowing that child was down there in the dirt. Alone. You couldn't stomach it.'

He looked down at the desk, closed eyes. When he raised his head and stared at Janine, he looked tired, cynical, his cheeks hollowed.

'We know about your brother. About Gary,' she said.

Joe Breeley jerked as if she had slapped him then sat back his eyes blinking rapidly, his face tight and Janine could see how close he was to breaking point.

'Oh you do, do you? You know all about that,' he said bitterly.

'He had a fractured skull, too. Same age. What happened this time, Joe? Another accident?'

Joe Breeley's mouth was rigid, his face pale. His upper body was shaking and Janine realised his leg was bouncing up and down as it had at the house. A nervous tic. He didn't answer.

'Who is he?' Janine said.

He looked down, put his head in his hands.

Janine spoke quietly. 'Someone out there is worried sick because their little boy is missing. You're a father. Imagine that? That little boy needs a name. We need to find out what happened to him and return him to the people who love him so they can lay him to rest.'

She kept pushing but keeping her tone soft, full of concern. 'Where he is, he's no name, no identity, like a bit of rubbish that no-one cares about. He has a mother, he has a father, they deserve the truth. That's all they can have now. That little soul needs peace. I think you do too.'

He raised his head, tears leaking from the sides of his eyes, anguish stretched across his face.

'Where did you find him? Who is he, Joe?'

He shook his head, raised his hands to his face, pressed his fingers against his lips as though he'd stop the words. Gave a sob.

'Joe, please, who is he?'

'He's my son.' His arms fell, he cried to the heavens. 'My boy. He's dead and he's my son.'

CHAPTER 26

'Is he losing it, or what? Has he got another kid?' Richard said as soon as they were alone, after the solicitor had insisted on a break and Janine agreed without argument. 'Is there a previous relationship?'

'Not that we know of,' Janine said. 'They've the baby — and John,' Janine recalled the photos, the child crying from upstairs. *Miserable with chickenpox.* 'And no-one's reported a child missing, anyway. Apart from Sammy. If he was from a previous relationship surely the mother would have . . . John Breeley's been sick,' she was thinking aloud, 'we didn't see him. We heard him though.'

She looked at Richard. Her stomach turned over and her bowels turned to water. 'We heard a child. We were told it was John.'

Richard narrowed his eyes, listening intently to her.

'There is a connection,' she said, her mouth dry and heart thumping. 'This is John, our victim. The child we heard upstairs — I think it's Sammy.'

The way Breeley had hesitated when Janine mentioned DNA. He must have thought then that they'd soon identify the relationship between father and son, that the game was up. That no matter how vehemently he denied all knowledge of the crime, the science would blow it all wide open.

'He killed his son and took Sammy?' Richard said.

'The timing would fit. He puts John there early Saturday morning, goes away and comes back just after nine. He works the morning. . .'

'Goes to the park,' Richard said.

'That's why we've had no reports of another missing child.' She could feel her pulse racing, a buzzing in her head.

'We arrest Mandy as an accomplice and remove the children,' she said.

'You sure?' Richard said.

'That it's Sammy? Hell, yes. This time I'm sure.' She was trembling with adrenalin but she needed to focus, to use the energy to concentrate on the task in hand — recovering Sammy from Mandy Breeley.

* * *

There was no reply at the house. Janine peered through the letter box, no sign of life, no sounds from upstairs. Shap checked around the back and found the same. They began knocking on doors along the street.

A neighbour opposite reported seeing Mandy leave with the children in the car only a few minutes earlier. She knew the family well and was able to tell them where Mandy's mother lived.

'Richard and I will go round there now,' Janine told the team who stood, poised to act, outside the Breeley's house with all the neighbours watching. 'Shap, flag up the car registration so we can try and catch her with ANPR if she's done a runner,' referring to the automatic number plate recognition technology they could use. 'Butchers, get onto telecoms, we want to pinpoint her location if she uses her phone — Joe Breeley will have her number in his. Be prepared to instigate a child rescue.'

Janine rang Lisa and brought her up to speed. 'Map out radius, probable distance travelled and time projections. Set up a child abduction alert. Shap will give you the details.'

Shap got out his phone. As Janine hurried to her car Shap began to speak to Lisa, 'Maroon Vauxhall Astra registration mother 635 x-ray, lima, hotel. Full alert all ports and airports. Occupants twenty-five-year old white female, long blonde hair, believed to be travelling with infant boy and three-year-old boy . . .'

* * *

Mandy's mother lived about a mile away and looked disconcerted when she opened the door to police officers.

'Have you seen Mandy today?' Janine asked her, once she'd identified herself.

'No.'

'Have you heard from her?'

'No. Why? What's going on?' she said.

Janine didn't have time to go into a full blown explanation so said instead, 'She's missing from home and we're anxious to speak to her.'

'About what? What on earth's the matter?' the woman's voice rose.

'I'm sorry, I can't discuss that with you now but please if you do hear from her will you let us know immediately?' Janine passed her a card. The woman opened and closed her mouth, her forehead creased, eyes bewildered.

Knowing what she did, Janine felt a moment's pity for Mandy's mother. Whatever happened in the hours to come, her life was about to be torn apart as she learnt about the death of her grandson and the abduction carried out by her son-in-law. 'I'm sorry,' Janine said, 'I have to go.'

They drove away, the woman still standing in her doorway, as if frozen by dread.

Janine requested that Joe Breeley be returned to the interview room.

He came in walking slowly, face drained of colour. He sat beside his solicitor and rubbed at his face with his palms, like he was trying to wake himself up.

'Joe, Mandy's missing,' Janine said.

'What about Aidan?' He looked alarmed.

'She's taken him, and Sammy.'

He froze and looked at her, he obviously hadn't realised they had made the connection. Did he think he could hide the abduction from them?

'I don't know anything about Sammy.'

Lying.

'Are you telling us you didn't abduct Sammy Wray?' Richard said.

'I didn't,' he said.

'We heard him at the house,' Janine said, 'remember?'

His face crumpled. He sniffed. 'I can't—'

The lone woman in the park. Janine's stomach fell. *Mandy!* Mandy, deranged with grief, had substituted someone else's child for her own. And Joe was trying to shield her.

'Mandy,' she said. He flinched, wouldn't meet her eye. 'We're very concerned for their safety. Where would she go?'

'You'll take him off her, Aidan.' He shook his head. 'You'll charge her. I can't do that to them.'

'And if it all goes wrong?' Janine said.

'No,' he said.

'If you help us, Joe, that will be taken into account,' Richard said.

'I don't care about that,' he exploded. 'Christ, do you think that matters?' He put his hands on his head, pulled at the hair there, his knuckles white.

'We need to contact her friends. Perhaps she's left the children with someone or asked somebody for help,' Janine said.

There was a long pause. He seemed torn. 'I can't,' he said eventually.

They examined his phone anyway and Shap began ringing round all the contacts in his list.

'Mandy went out shopping on Friday afternoon,' Janine said. The car broke down. You were on your own with the boys, tell me what happened.'

'It was an accident,' he said, his voice shaking. 'I just wanted him to stop messing about.' He shook his head.

'Joe?' she prompted, 'What was he doing?'

'He was having a tantrum, chucking his food all over the place, kicking me. He's screaming his head off. I pick him up and—'

He stopped short, lips crimped together, his fists clenched, miming how he held the child by the shoulders.

'You shook him?' Richard said.

'Yeah, and he's yelling and I just . . .I—'

'Go on,' Janine said.

He took a rapid breath in. 'I just put him down, too rough and he goes backwards, hard against the wall. Then he's quiet.' Breeley began to sob, his shoulders heaving, saliva at the corners of his mouth. 'She wouldn't let him go,' his distress was palpable, Janine felt her throat tighten.

'Why didn't you get help? Tell someone, if it was an accident?'

'They'd dredge it all up again — what's the chance of it happening twice? They'd never believe me. The truth. I told the truth back then and it all fell apart. Gary opened the cellar door, he'd not done that before. The light was broke but he didn't mind the dark. He must have tripped. It had gone quiet and I went to see what he was up to and the door was open.' He shivered. 'I didn't want to go down there. I got my bike lamp.'

Joe Breeley paused. Janine waited. Eventually he spoke again, his voice so low she had to lean in to catch it. 'He was still. He never kept still.' He rubbed at his face. 'My mam's eyes, her face — she never spoke to me again. I was ten years old. Fifteen years of wishing . . . Blame and hate — that's what the truth got me. And it never brought Gary back.' He looked at her, eyes lanced with pain. 'I loved my boy . . . I loved him . . . We sat with him all night. But I had to . . .'

'What did you do, Joe?' Janine said gently.

'I put him in the sheet, put him in the van. On the seat,' he added, 'not in the back, like.' The sad detail, as if he'd protect the child he had killed. Janine recalled Lisa's observation about the sheet being like a shroud. Perceptive.

'Then what?' she said.

'I drove to the house.'

'To 16 Kendal Avenue?' She had to have it all on tape, facts, figures, details.

'Yes. I got out of the van, opened the—' He stopped, overcome.

'Go on,' she said.

'Opened the manhole, I went for John. That's when my glasses broke.'

'You fetched John,' Janine prompted.

'I put him in the drain.' He was crying as he spoke, wiping at his face with his hands. 'I went home, came back just after nine.'

'And then after lunch, when you'd finished work, Mandy came home with Sammy?'

Joe Breeley shook his head sadly. 'I wanted John back,' he said, 'but it was too late.' His mouth worked.

He refused to tell them where Mandy might be. 'I can't,' he said, 'I can't do that to her.'

Eventually Janine and Richard withdrew but asked that Joe Breeley wait where he was, as they would certainly want to resume questioning him.

* * *

The incident room was alive with a sense of urgency. Phones were ringing and people taking calls in the background. A large map of the country, centred on Manchester, was projected onto an electronic whiteboard and Lisa had outlined circles with estimated time of travel.

'Butchers,' Janine said, 'speak to the bank, they're to notify us immediately if Mandy uses her cards.'

'The mobile network,' he said, 'say she's not calling anyone so far, phone's switched off.'

'If she's on the move, how far has she gone?' Janine said.

Lisa indicated on the map. 'Almost forty minutes, boss. She's somewhere in this area. No ANPR hits yet.'

'More than likely, she's on a motorway,' Janine said, 'cameras should be able to pick her up. Richard, we want a negotiator standing by. And talk to the National Crime Faculty — see if there's a psychologist can advise us on how to play it.' She turned back to Lisa. 'Are customs on board?'

'Yes, boss,' the young DC said.

'What about social services?'

'Will do.'

'We could go public, breaking news, I can get us a 'be on the lookout for,'' said Millie.

'Could freak her.' There was a moment's tension as Janine tried to weigh up whether this was the right tactic. 'OK,' she said, 'do it. But give me time to call the Wrays first.'

Millie left for the press office to set things in motion.

Shap called out, 'Breeley's contacts — no-one has heard from her in the last few days. No-one had any suggestion as to where we might find her.'

'Boss,' Lisa said, 'tea, coffee?'

'Yes, anything.' Janine was too bound up in the hunt to be able to make trivial decisions.

Janine rang Claire Wray, determined to warn her of unfolding events before she heard anything on the news. 'Claire, I wanted to let you know we have just received a strong lead as to Sammy's whereabouts and we're hoping to recover Sammy but I can't make any promises. As soon as I have any more information at all you will be the first to know.'

'You've found him?'

'We think we know where he's been held, I can't say more than that.'

'It's definitely Sammy?'

'We believe so,' Janine said. She couldn't be one hundred percent sure until she saw the child with her own eyes. She could hear Claire breathing but nothing else.

'Claire?'

'Is he alive?' Claire said.

'I believe so,' Janine said.

'But you don't know?'

'I can't be sure,' Janine said.

'But what—' Claire began.

'I'm sorry, I can't answer any more questions now. I'll be back in touch as soon as I can. Is Sue there?'

Janine briefed Sue, the family liaison officer, as quickly as she could. Then she let Lisa know the family had been informed of the breakthrough.

Lisa nodded, passed Janine a cup of tea. She took a sip, scalding her mouth, then Butchers called out, 'She's using her phone, she's on the phone.'

A mobile was chiming in among the office phones.

'Who's she calling?' Janine said.

Shap stood up, waving Breeley's handset. 'Joe. She's calling Joe.'

Janine snatched the phone and ran to the interview room. Janine handed Breeley the phone, 'Mandy calling' was on the display. She nodded for him to answer.

'Mandy?'

'Joe, I wanted to say goodbye. I had to go. I'm sorry.' Janine could hear her voice, distant, tinny, distraught.

'No, I'm sorry,' Joe Breeley said. 'It's my fault. It's all my fault. Come back, come home, please Mandy.'

'I love you, Joe. Remember that, I love you,' Mandy said.

'We can sort it out,' he answered, 'just come home. We can work something out.'

'It's too late. I'm sorry.'

'Mandy, no, don't!' Joe Breeley cried out.

But Mandy had ended the call.

'Oh, God,' he was agitated. 'Oh, Christ!'

'What does that mean,' Janine said, 'too late?'

He just sat there shaking his head.

'Joe,' said Janine, a cold feeling in the pit of her stomach, 'did Mandy make any threats?'

He pressed his knuckles against the edge of the table. 'When she brought him home, I said we'd have to take him

139

back, there'd be trouble. How long till people realised they'd not seen John, family, people in the avenue? She was all for a fresh start. Wait till the fuss died down and then move. I tried to make her see sense but she said if I took him away she'd . . . kill herself. She said life wouldn't be worth living anymore.'

CHAPTER 27

The first newsflash came over the television in the incident room. 'Police appeal for help in finding missing toddler Sammy Wray. Believed to be travelling with a woman and baby in a maroon Vauxhall Astra M635 XLH. Please ring this number if you see the vehicle or the occupants.'

'Got an ANPR hit,' Shap said.

'Where?' Lisa asked him.

'M62 West. Just past Warrington.'

Lisa typed in the details and pulled up a new projection on the whiteboard.

'She could be heading for Liverpool,' Shap said. He sent word to the boss who was still in with Breeley.

* * *

'Mandy's travelling towards Liverpool,' Janine said. 'We believe she may be trying to reach the airport or the port. Where's she going? Have you got family abroad. A place that's special?'

'What'll happen to Aidan?' Joe Breeley said.

'I don't know but let's get him back safe, yes?' Janine said.

'She wouldn't hurt him,' Breeley said but there was a hint of uncertainty in his voice.

'She's grieving. She's lost a child and taken a replacement. Mandy's on the run. She knows we've arrested you. The game's up. When things are that bad it can feel like there's only one way out. Are you willing to take that risk. With Sammy? With Aidan?' Janine spoke quietly, firmly. 'Too late, she said. But it needn't be.'

Joe Breeley hesitated, obviously torn.

'Come on, Joe. We need your help. Aidan needs your help. Wherever she is headed, she can't hide, not on her own, not with two children. I'm concerned for her safety and the children's safety. For Aidan.'

'I told you, she wouldn't hurt him,' he said.

'How can you be sure, she's never been in this situation before. She knows that we've arrested you, she probably understands it is only a matter of time before we work out what has happened. Where is she going?'

'I can't,' he said.

'It's better this way, believe me. You've already lost John, let's keep everyone else safe. Mandy can't do this on her own. She won't be thinking straight. She knows you've been arrested, she knows you'll be charged and remanded awaiting trial. You'll probably be convicted. You won't be there for her, the only thing you could do now is help us so we can reach her and bring them all back safe. Please help us do that.'

He shuddered, the motion shaking his shoulders and arms, rippling through his face. He put his hands to his head then said quietly, 'Isle of Man. She's cousins in Douglas. We used to talk about moving there. She thought it'd be a better place to bring up the kids.'

'Thank you. How do you usually get there?' Janine said.

'The ferry from Liverpool,' he answered.

* * *

142

Janine asked Richard and Butchers to remain with Joe Breeley and took Shap with her to try and intercept Mandy at the ferry.

'We should be with you in about thirty minutes,' Janine said to a contact in the port police. 'Mandy Breeley could be volatile. She's grief-stricken and she may be feeling desperate. We're faxing descriptions over for you. Let her board. Try not to do anything to spook her. Can you instruct your people not to approach her?' He agreed and assured her that the harbour master was prepared to delay sailing if necessary.

Shap was a good driver at speed and as the car raced along the M62 with an escort ahead to clear the traffic, Janine tried to ease the tension twisting in her guts. She wanted to be there now, faster, sooner. Her stomach was a heavy ball, her back stiff, even her fingers and toes felt locked, rigid. What if they were too late? Mandy's words: *Too late*. When the prospect of saving Sammy was in sight, what if it was snatched away? The Wrays would never survive that and Janine didn't think she would either.

She spoke to a hostage negotiator and gave him a summary of the situation. He said he'd meet them at the terminal as soon as possible but roadworks on his journey south might affect his expected arrival time.

At last the terminal came into view. They passed the cargo container depot with its massive stacks of metal boxes, followed the plethora of signage directing traffic to parking, loading and ferry-boarding areas. Overhead, gulls wheeled and shrieked and a fierce wind snatched at flags and litter. With their lights and sirens off, the unmarked cars drew up close to the ship itself.

Janine and Shap were greeted by the port police officer who was expecting them. Janine shook hands with him.

'We've done a discreet search,' he said, 'she's on the top deck. Coastguard standing by.'

'Thanks,' Janine said, 'social workers should be here anytime.'

'No negotiator yet?' he asked.

'On their way,' Janine said, 'the traffic's bad, an incident on the M6.' Janine didn't want to wait, felt that the outcome could be worse if they delayed and Mandy began to suspect something was wrong. She thought for a moment and then said, 'I know the situation. I've met her before. She might talk to me.'

He nodded.

'We go up,' she said, 'when I find her if we can clear that deck. . .'

'Sure, I'll brief these guys,' he nodded to his officers.

When everyone was clear on the strategy, Janine and Shap climbed the stairwells between the decks followed by the port officers. The ferry was busy with travellers: a stag party dressed in monkey outfits, families of all shapes and sizes, couples and solo travellers. Janine caught a whiff of hot fat and sugar from one of the cafés on board, mingled with the oily smell of diesel.

When they reached the top deck the wind was even fiercer. Janine saw Mandy at the far end, at the rail looking out to sea, Aidan in her arms, a baby feed and changing bag over her shoulder. Sammy was beside her, holding her hand. Sammy wore different clothes but had his red shoes on and his glasses.

Janine nodded and Shap with the port officers assisting him began to approach the other passengers and quietly ask them to go downstairs, making sure that no-one passed Mandy and alerted her to the evacuation. The wind helped them, masking the noise of people moving.

Soon they were alone and Janine walked closer to Mandy. She was perhaps ten yards away when Mandy turned, panic stark in her face as she caught sight of Janine. Mandy scooped up Sammy and began to retreat, edging along the perimeter of the deck.

'Mandy. Are you OK?' Janine said. She kept moving trying to narrow the distance between them.

'Go away,' Mandy said.

'We know about John,' Janine said, 'I am so sorry. You must miss him terribly.'

'He's fine,' Mandy glanced at the boy in her arms. 'Aren't you, love? We're fine. Just leave us alone.' The wind whipped at her hair.

'That's not John. That's Sammy. He hasn't been ill with chickenpox. He's sad and he's frightened and he misses his mum,' Janine said.

'I don't know what you're on about,' Mandy said.

'You saw him at the park. T-shirt just like John's. Same age, looked alike, that blonde hair. John had gone but you wanted him back. It hurt so much, didn't it?' Janine said.

Mandy started to cry.

'It can't work — a secret like that. That's Sammy, isn't it?' Janine said.

Mandy didn't speak, her mouth trembled.

'Mandy?'

The woman nodded, but she was still holding on tight to Sammy. She looked down at the freezing water. Janine's chest tightened. Janine didn't know enough about Mandy, about her history, her previous mental health, to know what she was thinking but given what Mandy had been through she must be disturbed. Anyone would be, to see her husband kill her first son, to have to relinquish him, to keep the ghastly deed a secret and play happy families whenever the police called round, to snatch Sammy and cope with the fear she must have felt every time someone came to the house.

'Joe told us what he did,' Janine kept talking, edging closer, keeping her voice as low as possible but fighting to be heard above the wind. 'You weren't there. You'd have stopped him. You love them. John and Aidan. I can see that. It was Joe, just Joe. He'd done it before.'

Mandy frowned.

'When he was a child himself. His brother. And now his boy,' Janine said. If she could just get her talking, interacting. Janine had done a basic course in hostage negotiation, you started by communicating, by interacting, by listening and empathising and enabling the person to open up to you.

'No. It's not like that,' Mandy said.

'Tell me,' Janine said.

'I wanted to get an ambulance,' Mandy said, 'to get help, but he wasn't moving.' Janine thought of her holding her child through that long, dark night. Feeling his lifeless body grow cold, then stiffen, the colour fade from his skin. Mandy hitched Aidan higher up on her shoulder. 'He just snapped, he's not a bad man, he has a temper but he's not a bad man. I was late back. Joe said we'd lose it all. With his brother, it was an accident, but they still put Joe in care, his mother left . . . Joe said he'd go down for it, and they'd take Aidan away . . . we'd lose everything . . . he was so sorry. Now, it's even worse — we've lost everything, anyway. There's nothing left.' Sammy began to grizzle and wriggled in her arms. She couldn't hold both children indefinitely.

Mandy, weeping, looked to the water again.

'Imagine if someone could bring John back?' Janine said. 'They can't, no-one can. But you can do that for Sammy's mum and dad. You can bring Sammy back for them. You know what it must be like for them, how sad they are. Please. Come with me now, Mandy. Come on. Please, Mandy. This is all a mess, but part of it we can put right. Part of it, you can make better.'

Mandy wept, snot on her face and tears damp on her cheeks. Around them the gulls called, their cries harsh and mocking.

'Please, Mandy.' Janine stepped closer, 'let me take Sammy.' Her mouth was dry, her heart in her throat. What if she misjudged it, lost all of them. 'I know you didn't want to hurt anyone. You were hurting. All you wanted was your little boy back, for things to be the same.'

Janine reached Mandy. Sammy was still crying quietly. 'That's it,' Janine said, soothing her as much as possible, 'that's it, I'll take Sammy, come on, that's it.' Janine put her hands round Sammy's waist. 'I've got him, come on Mandy,

that's it. Come on Sammy, there we go. I've got you, Sammy.'
Mandy relinquished her grip on Sammy and Janine lifted him
into her own arms. 'That's it. Good. It's all right.'

Mandy moved Aidan to the centre of her chest, wrap-
ping both her arms around him, kissing his head, her tears
falling on his fine blonde hair.

Janine turned to where the social workers waited near
the steps and nodded. One of them came up onto the deck
and approached them.

'Sammy?' she said.

Janine nodded.

'Hello, Sammy,' the woman said, 'off we go then, that's
it.' She took the child from Janine and walked back. Janine
waited until the clang of her shoes on the metal steps had
faded then put her arm around Mandy's shoulders. 'Let's go
down now. You give me your bag.'

Wordlessly, Mandy eased the bulky hold-all off her
shoulder and Janine took it. Gently she steered Mandy, one
arm on her back along to the steps and slowly guided her
down, the other officials melting out of the way.

Mandy froze when she saw the small crowd of people
waiting on the dockside at the end of the passenger walkway.

'It's all right, Mandy,' Janine said. The words were mean-
ingless, something to keep the woman walking, keep the child
safe. 'Come on.'

A woman with a name-tag on stepped forward and met
them as they stepped off the ship.

'Mandy,' she said, 'I'm Glenys, I'm Aidan's social worker.'

Mandy began to cry fresh tears.

'I know this is really hard but I will make sure that Aidan
is well looked after.'

'Can I see him?' Mandy cried.

'Yes, of course,' Glenys said, 'I'll arrange visiting as soon
as we have things straightened out. You're still his mum,
remember that, nothing can ever change that.'

The compassion brought a lump in Janine's throat.

'He'll want a bottle in an hour or so,' Mandy said through sobs like hiccups. 'There's a change of clothes in his bag. And his teddy. He likes rusks and apricot.'

Janine handed the bag to Glenys.

Glenys smiled at Mandy. 'Thank you.'

Mandy held her cheek against Aidan's head. 'Oh, baby,' she said, 'Oh, baby, I love you. Mummy loves you.'

Weeping helplessly she handed her son to Glenys.

'Mandy,' Janine said, 'I have to arrest you now.'

Mandy nodded, her chin quivering, wiping away her tears and snot with her hands, the wind still slapping at her hair. Janine began the caution, dimly aware of the passengers up on deck staring down at the unfolding drama.

CHAPTER 28

Janine accompanied Maria, the social worker, from the hospital where Sammy had been taken, back to the Wrays. She had informed the family liaison officer that Sammy would be coming home soon and asked her to prepare them, though how anyone prepared themselves for such a momentous change of fortune, was hard to imagine.

A press embargo was in place until Sammy was safely back with his parents, so the road outside the Wrays was deserted as they arrived. The rain had stopped at last. Millie wanted to organise a photo shoot for later that day, a batch of photographs to be taken by one of the official police photographers and made available to the media; something less intrusive than a scrum of press. Good news of this sort was rare in their work, on most occasions the best they could hope for was catching criminals, seeing them convicted for their crime but to have a child found safe and well after twelve days and reunited with their family was a happy outcome indeed. And excellent PR for the force, which would help counterbalance the wave of earlier hostile coverage.

Millie would also advise the Wrays on media interest. A bidding war for an exclusive was undoubtedly on the cards. It was the ultimate human interest story. They'd be handsomely paid if they agreed and very few families resisted that even if at first the idea seemed distasteful. What the money wouldn't do, couldn't do was fix the damage inflicted by the trauma of the abduction. In a lot of marriages and partnerships, relationships never survived that sort of pressure. Even when they did, the individuals were battered, bruised and scarred by the event, prone to emotional and mental illness, depression, PTSD, anxiety. She didn't know if the Wrays' marriage would survive. They obviously had their problems and Clive's behaviour at the outset had not shown him in a good light. But perhaps this 'happy ending' would give them a chance.

Janine undid Sammy's straps and helped him out of the child seat, lifting him out of the car.

Claire flew out of the door and ran down the path followed by Clive.

'Mummy!' Sammy, in Janine's arms, shouted, launching himself forwards. Claire took him from Janine, holding him tight. Clive ruffled Sammy's hair, kissed his cheek and led his wife and son to the house. Maria and Janine went in with them.

Sammy sat on Claire's knee and held on to his father's hand. Sue brought drinks and biscuits.

'He's been well looked after,' Maria told them. 'He's been checked out by a paediatrician and there are no worries at all.'

Claire nodded, her face mobile with emotion. Janine could see she was making a big effort not to break down in front of Sammy.

'I'll be here to support you over the next few weeks,' Maria said. 'You may find there are some different behaviours from Sammy as a result of what's happened. Trouble with sleep or regression we can deal with as needs be.'

'What sort of thing?' Claire said.

'It's common to have an apparent loss of skills, whether that is toilet training or language, dressing and so on. You may find he's clingy, watchful. You can help him by tolerating it. He needs to be with his primary carer as much as possible.'

Claire nodded.

'Try and reduce the number of times you separate for the time being,' Maria said. 'As for anxiety, avoid potential triggers, don't go to the same park for example.'

Claire shuddered.

'Routine is good,' the social worker went on, 'maintain any routine you had before. Sammy may become very angry for no apparent reason. If that happens it's important you keep calm; that will comfort him.'

'The woman,' Clive said, 'the one who took him.'

'She's in police custody,' Janine said, 'along with her husband.'

Clive shook his head. 'To do that—' he said.

Janine changed the subject. 'If the case comes to court, which is almost certain, then you may be called as witnesses.'

Claire gave a little moan, Sammy glanced at her quickly and she smiled to reassure him. Then Claire exchanged a look with Maria — she had seen how alert he was to her mood.

Hypervigilance, thought Janine, the term they used, a response to the trauma.

'It won't be for several months,' Janine said. 'And if they plead guilty then we won't have to go through the process of a trial.'

'Another biscuit,' Sammy said.

'Here.' Clive reached for the plate and Sammy picked up one, then glancing first at Clive and then at Claire, he took a second.

'Go on then,' Claire said, smiling, 'special treat.'

Janine told them about the photo shoot and then said, 'Is there anything else you want to ask me?'

Claire shook her head.

'I'll be on my way. Bye bye, Sammy.'

His mouth was stuffed with biscuit and he gave a little wave.

Clive got up and so did Claire.

'No, stay there,' Janine said, 'please. I can see myself out.'

'Thank you,' Claire said, a break in her voice, 'thank you so much.' Her eyes brimmed with tears.

'Yes,' said Clive.

Janine accepted their thanks, smiled and left them to it.

* * *

'CPS?' Louise Hogg said crisply.

'I'm preparing the file now and hope to speak to them early tomorrow. I think it's looking very promising.'

Hogg's eyebrows twitched as though she thought Janine's observation arrogant or overconfident. She looked back at Janine's interim report, turned a page, then closed the file.

Here it comes, Janine thought, the dressing down for last night. The questions about judgment and competency, about boundaries and professionalism. Had she mentioned Pete and Tina? She still couldn't remember.

'Anything else?' Hogg said.

'No, ma'am. If you're . . . erm . . . well, the team are having a drink, I'm popping in now.'

'Is that wise?' Hogg said.

Oh, God. Her heart sank. *Here it comes.* When Hogg didn't hold forth, Janine rallied. 'I'm on the fruit juice,' Janine said.

'No hair of the dog?' Was she joking?

'No. I'm driving,' Janine said.

Hogg nodded. 'I'll see this one out,' she said, 'give them my regards.'

'Thank you,' Janine turned to go, feeling the weight lift.

'Pint?' Shap said to Butchers.

'You buying?' Butchers said. He fancied a bevvy. They deserved to celebrate a job well done.

'Your turn, mate,' Shap said.

'Skint,' Butchers said, 'had to shell out for the do.' Just thinking about it made him uneasy.

'And nothing to show for it, apart from that black eye,' Shap said. 'I can sub you,' he offered. 'We could go on after, see about some action.' He winked.

'Get in!' Butchers scoffed.

'You should try the Internet,' Shap said, 'hundreds of birds on there looking for love.'

'Looking for trouble, more like,' Butchers said.

'Can't do worse than the lovely Kim.'

'She wasn't that bad,' Butchers said.

Shap stared at him.

Butchers shuffled. 'Mebbe she was,' he allowed.

Shap pulled on his ear and grimaced. 'Thing is,' he said, 'you've got to know what you're after.'

'Bit of peace and quiet'd do me,' Butchers said.

'She messed with your bearings, mate, didn't she? Mucked up your sense of judgement. Sent you banging on about Luke Stafford and Phoebe Wray.'

'With good reason,' Butchers objected.

'What reason?' Shap sneered. 'You were way off, mate, way, way off.'

'You coming,' Lisa called from the corridor, 'only neither of you stood me a round last night so it's your shout.'

CHAPTER 29

Claire felt jittery, her pulse racing, thirst raging. She fought to appear calm for Sammy.

Once the photographer had been and gone and the social worker and the family liaison officer had left, obviously delighted by the happy event, the three of them were alone together.

When she wondered how it had been for Sammy, away from home, in a strange house, without his toys or books or anything familiar, in the presence of a man who had killed his child, her heart ached and burned. A swarm of questions hummed in her mind but she had been advised to let Sammy talk at his own pace, if he chose to talk. And that the best care they could give was to re-establish all the routines he knew.

So with her heart fluttering, Claire asked him if he'd rather have egg and soldiers or beans on toast and then, when he said beans she went to make them while Sammy sat watching television nestled on Clive's lap.

And after tea, Clive took him up for a bath and it was all she could do not to run up there and watch. She wanted him in sight, in earshot, every moment.

Resisting that impulse and eager for distraction, she stripped and changed their double bed and then cleaned the fridge.

Clive brought Sammy down, pink-cheeked, his curls damp and honey coloured from the water.

'I've just spoken to Phoebe,' Clive said, 'she'd like to see him.'

Claire's first reaction was hot defiance but as she took a breath to rebuff the idea Clive said steadily, 'She's been worried, too. She'd like to see her brother. I said it would only be for a few minutes, near bedtime.'

'You said yes?' He'd already arranged it.

'Yes.' Clive turned to Sammy, chucked him under the chin. 'You remember Phoebe?'

Sammy gave a nod.

'She's coming to say hello.'

Clive set Sammy down on the sofa and then looked at Claire. 'No more messing about, no hiding,' he said quietly. 'It's a new start.'

She wasn't sure what she felt but she wasn't going to make a scene about it. And she felt herself relax a little, the tension ease across her shoulders.

* * *

Sammy played with his dinosaurs and Claire watched, alert for any change to his actions or his commentary, keen to find any clues as to the differences he'd encountered but there was nothing new or unusual in what he did.

His face lit up when Phoebe arrived, which astonished Claire. They had only met once before. But Phoebe had an easy way with him and kept up a stream of chatter and Sammy insisted on showing her all his special things, bringing one item after another, taking Claire with him to fetch them each time (Tyrannosaurus, my big stone, the red digger, baby mouse) until the floor was littered with them.

'Bedtime now,' Clive said and Phoebe left promptly, kissing Sammy on the cheek, hugging her father and thanking Claire on her way out.

Claire had an image of Phoebe coming round to babysit for Sammy and the new baby and felt her eyes sting with tears at the prospect of normality and the rift between Clive and Phoebe healing.

She took Sammy up to bed. He insisted on counting each step like he did. In his room she sat beside him on the bed, and read the customary two books.

He took his glasses off, put them on his bedside table and pulled his teddy bear close, burying his nose in the fur.

'Night, night, lovely boy,' Claire said but she stayed there, listening to Sammy's breathing, gazing at him until her eyes closed and she sank into sleep.

Clive woke her a little later, shaking her shoulder, whispering her name.

'I'm going to sleep here tonight,' she said.

He looked worried.

'Just tonight,' she said, 'I promise.'

And he accepted that and when he bent to embrace her, she was happy for it. 'We're so lucky,' she said quietly.

'We are,' he said, 'I love you.'

'Yes,' she knew he did. 'I love you, too,' she said. And she knew that for the first time in weeks she meant it.

CHAPTER 30

Richard was removing items from the incident boards when Janine came in. The rest of the team were having a well-earned beer. Hair of the dog for some. But tomorrow they'd be back in early, putting together all the reports needed to build the case for trial.

She thought he might congratulate her on a good out-come, no further loss of life but all he said was, 'Reckon they'll prosecute her?'

'Hard to say. I'm not pushing for it. More good would come of letting her raise that baby.'

'And Breeley?' Richard said.

'He caused John's death — then he covered it up. Put his son's body in a drainage tunnel,' Janine sighed. 'If he'd come clean straight away, things might have been different.'

Millie came in then, her coat on. Nodded to them both.

'Five minutes?' Richard said.

'Fine.' Millie turned to Janine, 'Congratulations. Great copy.'

'Thanks,' Janine said. The shadow of the previous evening still made her embarrassed.

'See you down there,' Millie said to Richard.

Once Millie had gone, Richard took down the remaining items and put them in the box files. He picked up his jacket and laptop.

Janine didn't want him to go without trying to make the peace. 'Last night,' she said, 'I was out of order. Everything—' she stopped herself from trying to justify her behaviour. 'No excuse.'

'No,' Richard agreed.

'I'm sorry,' she said.

'Maybe you should tell that to Millie,' he said unsmiling.

'I will. She's coming for a drink?'

'Yes.'

'I'll talk to her,' Janine said.

'OK.' He put his jacket on and walked to the door.

'But there is something.'

'What?'

'Not an excuse, more a sort of explanation with a big apology attached. I was kicking the cat. I know you don't really get it, the baby thing but it's . . . let's just say that for me it's a biggie. I was struggling and you seemed a million miles away, not even on my side anymore and Millie, well, she seemed to be the reason. But I was unfair and I was a cow and I'm really sorry. It was just with Pete and Tina—' She sighed, began to close down her files. 'She's nice.'

'Tina?'

'No, not Tina, Tina is a bloody nightmare. Millie.'

'I know.'

'I'm still not convinced,' Janine murmured.

'What's that?' he stopped.

'That she's your type.'

'I don't have a type.' Richard took the bait, a glimmer of mischief in his eyes. 'What's my type? Go on.' He was laughing. Almost.

'You're going to be late,' Janine said and turned back to her screen.

She would join the team, down a tonic without the gin or maybe an orange juice. And then she'd head off. Home to her kids.

158

She might put off explaining about the divorce until there was a bit more time to field questions and deal with the inevitable upset. But she'd tell them that it would be OK. Pete could still have them every other weekend and holidays. The baby would come along and everything would change a little bit but life would go on.

She saved her files and powered down the computer.

We'll be fine she'd tell them — don't worry.

Janine paused at the door, looked back at the notice boards which looked bare now, vacant.

We did it, she thought. After all that mess and confusion we did it. Solved the murder and found the missing child. John could be laid to rest and Sammy was back with his mum and dad. We did it, she thought, as she snapped off the lights. We bloody did it!

THE END

ACKNOWLEDGEMENTS

Thanks to everyone involved with *Blue Murder* at Granada and especially to Anna Davies — a brilliant script editor.

ALSO BY CATH STAINCLIFFE

DETECTIVE JANINE LEWIS MYSTERIES
Book 1: BLUE MURDER
Book 2: HIT AND RUN
Book 3: MAKE BELIEVE

Thank you for reading this book.

If you enjoyed it please leave feedback on Amazon or Goodreads, and if there is anything we missed or you have a question about, then please get in touch. We appreciate you choosing our book.

Founded in 2014 in Shoreditch, London, we at Joffe Books pride ourselves on our history of innovative publishing. We were thrilled to be shortlisted for Independent Publisher of the Year at the British Book Awards.

www.joffebooks.com

We're very grateful to eagle-eyed readers who take the time to contact us. Please send any errors you find to corrections@joffebooks.com. We'll get them fixed ASAP.

Lightning Source UK Ltd.
Milton Keynes UK
UKHW010935090922
408600UK00002B/369